Briarwood Cottage

JoAnn Ross

New York Times bestselling author JoAnn Ross returns to Shelter Bay's sister city, Castlelough, Ireland, home to her beloved, award-winning Irish trilogy—*A Woman's Heart, Fair Haven, and Legends Lake*—with a story about a woman overcoming tragedy and a man whose heart she once broke.

When burned-out war journalist Duncan McCaragh is assigned to cover a "sighting" of the Lady, Ireland's sea beastie version of Scotland's Nessie, he decides to use his forced time in Castlelough to come up with a plan to win back his estranged wife. Failure is not an option…

What he has no way of knowing is that photojournalist Cassandra Carpenter is also on her way to Castlelough with the divorce papers Duncan's been refusing to sign. Can the magic of the Emerald Isle and the Lady reunite these two wounded hearts?

1

DUNCAN MCCARAGH HAD always trusted his instincts, which had kept him alive more times than he cared to count.

When Diane—the stylish brunette executive assistant who'd flirt a bit whenever he came to Manhattan—kept her gaze glued to her computer screen while he cooled his heels in the outer office of the Global News Network, his Spidey senses began to tingle.

Duncan had survived an IED explosion in Iraq, a firefight in the Hindu Kush, and had sweated bullets convincing a Syrian military officer that he was merely a correspondent in the country covering the civil war. He'd had his phone confiscated during his brief imprisonment but had lived to tell the tale.

Over the years, some had called him brave. Others, who envied his knack for being in exactly the right place at the right time, claimed he was merely lucky. Still others, mostly his competitors, insisted that his earlier military deployments had made him a reckless adrenaline junkie who was like a dog with a bone when it came to never giving up on a story. Hence the nickname Mad Dog

McCaragh.

The sudden buzz of the intercom shattering the hushed silence caused a flare of heat in his chest. Diane picked up the receiver, cast a quick, unreadable glance his way, then said, "Yes, sir."

She hung up. "He'll see you now." The sympathy in her intelligent brown eyes was not encouraging.

Steeling himself for the verbal whiplashing he knew would be coming, Duncan rubbed the heel of his palm against the fire burning beneath his ribs, then walked down the long hallway appropriately painted the threatening gray of the sky just before a storm.

The man in the custom-tailored suit sitting on the other side of the heavy antique desk didn't bother to look up as Duncan waded across the thick pewter carpet.

Although his nerves were nearly as tangled as they'd been during that Syrian strip search, and the lingering remnants of a hangover had him feeling as if terrorists were shooting rockets into his head, Duncan kept his face neutral and his eyes directed straight ahead.

"So, Duncan." After what seemed a lifetime, Winston Armstrong III finally put down the gold pen he'd been signing papers with, braced his elbows on the top of the desk, and linked his fingers together. "Would you care for something to drink? Coffee? Water?"

He did not, Duncan noticed, offer the single malt Scotch from the bar hidden behind one of the bird's-eye maple wall panels.

"I'm fine. Thank you." If you ignored a jaw as stiff as the suspension on the Humvees he'd bounced around in during deployments in Iraq and Afghanistan.

"Well, then." The president and CEO of GNN slanted

his head. Looking hard. Looking deep. "Why don't you sit down? And take off the damn glasses. I prefer to look a man in the eyes when I'm speaking to him."

"I'd just as soon stand." And face the firing squad straight on, like a man. But Duncan did pull off the shades.

The older man sighed heavily as he took in the blooming black eye the glasses had been concealing. "Why do you always have to make everything so damn difficult?"

Never one for introspection, Duncan had, actually, been asking himself that same question since returning Stateside. And hadn't managed to come up with a satisfying answer. "I guess it's my nature."

"Your father's a tough man," his employer and godfather allowed, telling Duncan nothing he didn't already know himself.

"Dad comes from a long line of pirates."

Duncan's family financial roots went back to an ancestor who'd been one of the original founders of the Philadelphia Stock Exchange. Established in 1790, it was the oldest stock exchange in the country. Duncan had been invited to join the exclusive club but had found even the dog-eat-dog, winner-take-all mentality of trading too tame for his liking.

He'd also never found the idea of making money for money's sake the least bit appealing. Having been on the go since he'd dropped out of Princeton the second semester of his junior year to join the Marines, Duncan figured if it didn't fit in a duffle bag and backpack, he didn't need it.

"James can be ruthless," Armstrong agreed. "But he's never been self-destructive."

"And you're saying I am?"

"You've taken unnecessary risks."

"Excuse me," he said through gritted teeth. "But despite the phone and tablet chargers they've installed at the tables, it'd be a little difficult to do my war correspondent's job from a booth at The Breslin."

Okay. That might not have been the brightest thing to say. The Breslin Bar & Dining Room was one of Manhattan's top power restaurants. It was also Armstrong's favorite watering hole.

"True," the older man said with that all-too-familiar patrician tone Duncan would be subjected to whenever he managed to make it back home for a family holiday dinner. "Just as it would be difficult for me to ensure continued sponsors to fund your globetrotting from some godforsaken outpost on the Pakistani border."

"Point taken." Duncan knew that he was fortunate to even have work these days. Recently he'd watched more and more fellow correspondents forced to polish up rusting resumes and learn to blog after their newspapers had closed down or their network gigs outsourced to indie news-gathering operations.

"You do realize that it was only my call to the police commissioner that kept you from landing in jail after that bar brawl?"

"It wasn't a brawl." Exactly. Giving up, Duncan threw his body into one of the leather chairs on the visitor's side of the desk. "And I paid the damages."

"You took on five sailors the first day of Fleet Week. *Five.* I'd say that's pretty much setting yourself up for a less-than-positive outcome."

The sailors in question, who, despite having spent a

good part of the day and night trying to drink New York dry, had recognized him immediately. And instead of being impressed, they'd accused him of belonging to some elite media club that slanted news to its own chickenshit antiwar agenda.

Which was when his temper, admittedly fueled by alcohol, had flared. Duncan might not always approve of the way wars were run, but *no one* could accuse him of not respecting the men and women sent out to fight those wars. Especially since he'd been one of them.

He was a Marine. One of the Few. The Proud. The Brave.

Not some squid sailor who spent deployments sleeping on a comfy rack, taking daily hot showers, and eating steak in the "dining facility" (the chichi name that had replaced Mess Deck) while he'd been wolfing down MREs between mortar attacks in the godforsaken Afghan mountains.

"Since you now essentially have both police and Naval targets on your back, I assured the commissioner and police chief, not to mention the responding MAs, that you'd leave town for the remainder of Fleet Week," Armstrong said.

The trio of Master of Arms (MPs in the Marines, but for some freaking reason the Navy had to be different) had managed to take control of the situation before New York's finest arrived on the scene. The fact that they'd been the size of giant sequoias had added to their authority.

"My bags are packed." They always were. "So, I'm guessing the Middle East." The one region of the world that could always be counted on for a story.

"Not this time."

"I've always liked the blintzes at the Moscow Marriott's brunch." The hotel, located in the center of the city, on the edge of Red Square close to the Kremlin, was where high-ranking Russian government types tended to hold conferences and drink. Which led to a lot of breaking stories.

"You're getting closer." Armstrong leaned back in his chair, obviously enjoying dragging this out. "Try Ireland."

Duncan narrowed his eyes as he considered that surprise. "The Troubles have started up again?"

A silver brow arched. "Did I say *Northern* Ireland? You're going to the Republic."

"What's happening there?"

"You're the correspondent. Isn't it your job to tell me?"

"I'm a *war* correspondent. Unless Great Britain has decided to take Ireland back again, I can't see what I'd be covering."

"There's been a sighting of the Lady."

Damn. Duncan rubbed the scraped and bruised knuckles of his left hand. "You're not talking about the Virgin Mary."

"Nope. The Lady you'll be covering is in Castlelough, on the west coast. The same one depicted in Quinn Gallagher's horror novel. And the Academy Award-winning movie."

"That's fiction." He'd read the book and seen the movie about the mythical lake creature that was Ireland's answer to Scotland's Nessie.

"So some say. Others believe otherwise."

"Tracking down tabloid stories isn't my beat."

Though it did appear to be what his estranged wife was forced to cover these days. Duncan suspected Cassandra hated writing about alien abductions as much as he would. Of course, she wouldn't have to stoop to such tripe if the frustratingly stubborn female would only spend some of the money he deposited into her bank account every month.

"Your beat is what I say it is. But you have a choice." Armstrong picked up a blown-glass globe paperweight and began moving it from hand to hand. "You can go to Ireland or take a two-month leave of absence. You are, after all, long overdue for a break."

Two freaking months? After ten years spent in places that most people probably couldn't even find on a map, Duncan might not be the idealist he'd once been. And the adrenaline boosts from being in the midst of a battle were proving more and more elusive. But that didn't mean he'd have a clue what to do with himself for sixty long days. And even longer nights. Nights that were mostly spent thinking of the one woman he'd never been able to get out of his mind.

"I could quit."

"You could." The older man didn't appear to be quaking in his Gucci oxfords at that prospect. "But here's where I remind you that your contract has a no-compete clause. Which would essentially put you out of the news reporting business for a year."

"I'll take two weeks," Duncan countered.

He couldn't remember the last time he'd taken a vacation. Even his delayed honeymoon, coincidentally spent in Ireland to coincide with an EU conference held to address the burst of the country's property bubble, had been cut short by violent fractures in the democratic hopes born of the Arab spring.

"Six weeks," Armstrong returned.

"Three."

"Four. And that's my final offer. And I'm also assigning you to send back four human-interest stories about the Lady to end the evening newscast on consecutive Fridays.

"You're not serious." Duncan's vision of hell had always been spending eternity forced to do saccharine reports about high school sweethearts finding each other again on Facebook after seventy-five years apart and the birth of baby pandas.

"As a heart attack. Take it or hand over your credentials and go home."

Which they both knew Duncan couldn't do. Because, other than the Manhattan apartment where he occasionally landed between assignments, he had no real home. Life was, and had been for years, on the road.

"You realize, of course, that this is going to be a total waste of my time and your money."

The closest thing to a smile he'd seen thus far, or perhaps it was a smirk, twitched at the corner of Armstrong's mouth. "Fortunately, I happen to have the money. And you *will* make the time."

Four weeks. Hell, he'd survived worse situations in worse places for a lot longer than that.

"Sold," he said with a shrug. One thing Ireland had that Afghanistan and the Middle East had been sorely lacking was a plethora of pubs.

"I'm glad you agreed."

Armstrong reached into the middle desk drawer and pulled out an airline folder and a small manila envelope.

"Diane reserved a seat for you on tonight's Aer Lingus flight to Shannon. Although the town's swarming with Lady seekers, she also used her considerable powers of persuasion to book you a place to stay. You can pick up the key at Brennan's Pub in Castlelough. I'm assured you can't miss it, since, according to the Google map printout Diane included, it's in the center of town right across from the harbor."

After leaning forward to take the folder, Duncan glanced inside at the e-ticket and travel information. "Briarwood Cottage?" He didn't bother to hide his distaste.

"I realize it's not your usual level of five-star accommodations. But this is last-minute. And beggars can't be choosers."

He could choose not to go. For a fleeting moment, Duncan considered that throwing his press badge onto that gleaming desk would be preferable to covering a ridiculous tabloid story from some rundown wreck of a thatched-roof cottage that was probably filled with shamrock and leprechaun kitsch.

Having always been a realist, Duncan reluctantly decided that even tacky ceramic leprechauns would be better than losing his job and—God help him—having to take up blogging.

"I'll go."

"Good." The older man's self-satisfied smile assured Duncan that he'd expected no other outcome.

Duncan was halfway to the door when Winston Armstrong's next statement stopped him in his tracks. "And while you're over there in the back of beyond, figure out what you're going to do about your marriage. Before you spiral down so far you end up living in the subway."

"My marriage is *my* business."

"I'd define it as a *lack* of a marriage," Armstrong countered. "And, as your godfather, I'm not about to remain silent while you destroy your life. Not to mention disappointing your father."

"I've been doing that pretty much my entire life."

"You're mistaken about that. But you've got a trip to take, so we'll save the discussion for another time. Even if you don't care about winning approval, Duncan, perhaps at least you wouldn't want to break your mother's heart."

Damn. "That's hardball," Duncan muttered.

"I didn't get where I am by playing beanbag." Armstrong sighed heavily. "Look, it's obvious that your personal problems are affecting your work. So, do whatever the hell it takes. But get your head straight, Duncan. Before it's too late."

In no mood to argue that his Fleet Week reaction was just a temporary glitch, that those sailors had managed to jerk his chain during a time he'd just as soon forget, Duncan merely snapped a brisk salute.

Then walked out the door, down the hall, and out of the office, taking the elevator to the lobby, where a black car, right on cue and obviously already ordered by Winston Armstrong's ever-efficient Diane, glided up to the curb.

As he sat at the gate, waiting for his flight to Shannon Airport, Duncan idly watched the departing flights flash by on the oversized screen. When a pending flight to Portland, Oregon, caught his eye, he was tempted to ditch his trip and head off to the Pacific Coast instead. He could rent a car in Portland and be in Shelter Bay, Oregon, in two hours.

Absently rubbing the gold band he continued to wear on his left hand, he rationalized that he would, after all, be getting out of the city, as instructed. And, rationalizing the idea even more, the man he'd known all his life had told him to get his head straight and fix his marriage.

Which he damn well couldn't do in Ireland.

But just maybe...

The Portland flight turned out to be filled with a long list of standbys. Which wasn't as much of an obstacle for him as it would be for the ordinary traveler. Duncan's fame, along with the fact that he'd garnered more frequent flier miles than he'd ever be able to use in several lifetimes, would easily get him bumped to the front of the line and into someone else's seat.

He was considering doing exactly that when the boarding announcement for the Shannon flight came over the loudspeaker.

Reminding himself that his impulsiveness hadn't exactly won him points in his short-lived marriage, nor in that Midtown bar, and since there was no way he was going to waste time talking to crazy people who'd supposedly seen some imaginary lake creature, Duncan decided he might as well use his four weeks in the Emerald Isle to plan the mission to win back his runaway bride.

2

APPARENTLY OREGONIANS HADN'T received the memo that most people—at least most *normal* people—didn't go to the beach on chilly, foggy days. Cassandra had come here to be alone, to attempt to quiet the mental clatter in her mind and savor the smallest of things while they lasted. Such as the iridescent bubbles shimmering in sea foam washing up on the sand, the skittering of sandpipers along the water's edge, and the feel of the salt-scented breeze on her face.

There'd been a time, not so long ago, when she'd been so lost in the shadowed corners of her mind that she never would have been able to share the early-morning beach with runners, beachcombers, surfers, and even a group of young men practicing kite-flying stunts for the town's annual festival this upcoming weekend. A time when Cassandra's heart had been so consumed with pain there'd been no room for any other emotion.

But as she watched the crayon-bright colors of the soaring, dancing, diving kites providing a vivid contrast to the quilted gray sky, she felt as if they were lifting her spirits up with them.

Until a surfer clad in a skintight black wetsuit strode out of the water, his board beneath his arm. With his long blond hair and thin, seal-sleek body, the young man was the physical opposite of Duncan McCaragh, yet he nevertheless brought back a bittersweet memory of surfing beneath a full moon on County Donegal's Bundoran Beach.

Although she'd insisted he was living up to his Mad Dog name by even considering surfing in Ireland in the winter, Duncan had assured her that Irish waves were the best in winter. A declaration with which all the wet-suited people who'd shown up at Ireland's surf capital appeared to agree.

Using his considerable charm, he'd coaxed her into renting a board and clothing at one of the local shops. Having never surfed, Cassandra wouldn't have managed to stand up had it not been for Duncan's strong arms around her body, holding her up. Which had been no hardship.

Afterwards, they'd driven over the mountains to the west, where they'd spent ten idyllic days and romantic nights in a pretty little whitewashed, thatched-roof cottage before they were jerked back to reality and flew off in different directions. Duncan to Syria. Cassandra to Egypt.

Where everything had gone so terribly wrong.

At one time, just thinking about her estranged husband would bring on a surge of lust. Now, guilt, that other nagging emotion, descended, as cold and thick as the fog swirling in from the sea as Cassandra made her way back toward the cliff steps.

She'd nearly reached the steps when two little girls and a boy dressed in bright jackets came racing down. The boy had a dachshund on a leash.

The children's parents—the mother carrying a small, insulated cooler, the father laden down with folding chairs—had fallen behind. From midway up the cliff, they called out warnings for the kids to be careful. And wasn't that what every parent wanted for their children?

The happy, carefree family should have lifted Cassandra's spirits. There'd been a time when it would have. But she'd discovered over these past months that grief and guilt could came in waves just when you weren't expecting it. Like now, as memories crashed back, flooding over her like a tsunami. The children's laughter, as bright and cheerful as the kites flying overhead, caused her chest to tighten even as her heart galloped wildly.

Breathe.

Not sure her legs would hold her and unwilling to risk humiliating herself by publicly passing out, she sank down onto a driftwood log and pressed her hand against her galloping heart.

The parents paused as they passed. "Are you all right?" the woman asked solicitously.

"I'm fine," Cassandra lied through lips that had gone as dry as the sand beneath her feet. *Breathe.* She forced a smile that felt more like a grimace. "I guess I'm just out of shape. I walked too far down the beach, forgetting that I'd have to walk back."

"I've done that," the woman, who looked as if she did yoga during the day and Pilates in her sleep, answered with a friendly smile. "Of course, keeping after those three wild ones builds stamina. Which I'm going to need in spades this fall when the latest member of the brood arrives."

She absently patted the visible baby bump beneath her lightweight jacket as she glanced toward her brood. The girls had wasted no time in beginning a sand castle while the boy raced along the hard-packed sand at the surf line with the dog. "Well, have a good rest of your day," she said.

"Thanks. You, too."

Standing up, Cassandra made her way slowly up the steps, holding on to the railing with sweaty hands to steady herself. When she finally reached the car, she leaned back against the headrest and closed her eyes.

TWENTY MINUTES LATER, having nearly rid her mind of the ceaseless circling of what-ifs, Cassandra was approaching the bridge crossing the harbor into Shelter Bay when the radio's top-of-the-hour newscast led with her husband's name.

Expecting the worst, her heart, which had leaped into her throat, settled back down again when she learned that he hadn't been killed or injured in some godforsaken war zone. But instead had been involved in a drunken brawl in New York City.

During Fleet Week? Her Duncan?

No, Cassandra reminded herself. He wasn't *hers* anymore.

Despite the stubborn man's continued refusal to sign the divorce papers she'd sent him and that money that kept appearing every month in her bank account, their marriage was over.

Needing to know more, she pulled the car over to the side of the road, took out her phone, and Googled his name. Unsurprising, more than eleven million results popped up in twenty-five seconds.

After reading a half-dozen articles all claiming that he'd been banished by his news organization to Ireland, of all places, she clicked out of the search. She didn't want to think about her husband.

At. All.

And wasn't that easier said than done? Was it possible that this time the gossip columnists and the Twitterverse, not known for diligent fact checking, had gotten it right? Had Duncan truly been publicly drunk? And brawling?

They may not have spent that much time together during their brief marriage, but one thing Cassandra had always admired was her husband's ability to avoid unnecessary altercations. He'd told her that when your job required dealing with terrorists, dictators, and corrupt government officials, it was only prudent not to make unnecessary enemies.

Not that she hadn't witnessed a sustained intensity switch he was able to turn on at a moment's notice. And while he'd kept it tightly controlled, it wasn't anything anyone would want to have turned against them.

Her husband was as famous for his charm as he was that tightly leashed emotion. Also, having a socialite mother who was a closeted alcoholic had kept him careful about his drinking.

So, how had he ended up in a drunken brawl? With sailors?

Tucking the phone back into her bag, she continued driving across the bay to her cousin's apartment over Take the Cake Bakery.

"How was your walk?" Sedona Sullivan was sitting at

her kitchen computer going through yet another series of spreadsheets. Cassandra suspected she was one of very few bakers who did profit and loss analyses before deciding whether to add scones to her menu. Which was even more ironic given that her cousin had grown up on a commune.

"It was relaxing." Until that out-of-the-blue panic attack.

"I'm glad to hear that." Sedona glanced up from the screen. "So why are you as pale as driftwood?"

"I had a flashback," Cassandra admitted. "From what Dr. Fletcher would call a trigger. But it didn't last long."

"You were told it would take a while."

"I know. And I've read enough studies on PTSD to know it's unrealistic of me to expect a miracle cure. But it's getting better." At least she no longer felt as if she were viewing the world through a cracked, fogged-up lens. "Thanks to you for having given me this place to hide out."

"To reboot," Sedona suggested gently. "You're doing so much better than when you first arrived, Cass. You seemed to be having a good time at Bon Temps the other night."

"I was."

When Sedona had first rescued her from the dark cave that had become her life, Cassandra had spent the flight from New York to Portland bundled in blankets with a sleeping mask over her eyes to avoid having to speak to anyone.

Gradually, over these past weeks, her cousin had introduced her to various women friends gradually, one at a time, until she'd finally been able to join the group for dinner at the local Cajun restaurant and dance hall.

Although she hadn't danced, she *had* joined in the lively girl conversation and enjoyed her spicy shrimp jambalaya. Which was another change. When she'd first arrived, all her senses had been so numb she'd been existing mostly on a watery chicken soup delivered from the corner deli takeout. What was the point in eating when nothing had any flavor?

Of course, living with a baker who'd actually won ten thousand dollars on *Cupcake Wars* had helped her appetite to return. As had her more recent daily exercise. She'd been doing so well. Until that moment at the beach steps when everything had come crashing back...

Give it time, she repeated her therapist's advice. *Concentrate on how far you've come.*

"I had a thought driving back from the beach," she said.

"Oh?"

"As much as being together again has been like old times, I decided that I've taken advantage of your hospitality long enough," she said.

"You're leaving? Where to?"

"Ireland." She shared what she'd heard on the radio and read online.

"From what you've told me about Duncan, that doesn't sound like him at all."

"No. It doesn't. But on the drive back from the beach, I decided I've been living in limbo too long and I'll never be able to entirely move on if I don't deal with my marriage." Or lack of one.

"I think that's a great idea." Even as she voiced her enthusiasm, Sedona appeared uncharacteristically uncomfortable. "There's something you should know before you go," she said. "Something I've been holding back about the reason I showed up in New York in the first place."

"You said you'd wanted to look at the new spring fashions on Fifth Avenue and see the daffodils in Central Park's Conservatory Garden."

"I did say that." She sighed. "But the real reason I came when I did was because Duncan called me."

"Duncan called? When?" And wasn't this just a day of surprises?

Though, Cassandra belatedly realized, Sedona never had gone shopping. Nor, as far as she knew, to the park.

"The day he left the apartment. He said you were adamant about him leaving and was afraid that if he refused, you two would get into a big argument, which would only add to the stress and pain you were already dealing with. But he didn't want you to be alone, so he asked me to come to New York and stay with you. Or better yet, bring you back here."

"You lied to me?"

Cassandra belatedly realized that Sedona's timing had been too coincidental and her behavior too spontaneous for a former accountant who, if she had a flaw, it was that she tended to over-analyze everything.

"There's something else."

"I'm almost afraid to ask."

"He's called every week since then. The only time he missed was last month when he was deep in Taliban country and couldn't pick up a cell signal. He finally ran into a SEAL team and used their satellite phone to check in."

"What?" Cassandra was stunned. "How could you have kept that huge a secret for so long?"

"Believe me, it wasn't easy. And my only excuse, as weak as it might sound right now, is that when you arrived back to the States from the Middle East, you were so emotionally fragile."

Cassandra couldn't deny that. "I've gotten stronger. Yet you still kept your and Duncan's subterfuge from me."

"It wasn't exactly my choice, but every time I've tried to bring his name up, you've steadfastly refused to talk about him."

Another thing she couldn't deny. Damn.

She dragged her hand through her still unfamiliar short hair.

A few weeks ago, after finally noticing her long, lank, unwashed hair in the mirror, Cass had impulsively whacked away at it with a pair of Sedona's cooking shears. When her cousin had returned from selling cupcakes, instead of freaking out, she'd calmly called a stylist at the Cut Loose salon, who'd come over to the apartment and rescued the long strands from the bathroom wastebasket.

"It's so hard to find virgin hair these days," the woman, whose own spiky hair was bright fluorescent blue, had said with a warm smile. "You're going to make the people at Locks of Love very happy."

Then she'd gotten busy with her scissors and razor and ten minutes later, looking ever so pleased with herself, she'd declared the new short style a success.

"You look just like Tinkerbell."

Cassandra hadn't felt like Tinkerbell. Though, the prospect of going to Never Never land and never having to grow up, was admittedly appealing. Unfortunately, she was too late for that. "I want to be angry with you."

"I'd be angry and hurt if I were in your place, too," Sedona said. "If it makes any difference, I've felt miserably guilty. But I promise that I haven't broken any confidences about your life or anything you've shared with me. I've only reassured him that you're doing better every day."

"In large part because of that therapist you nagged me into seeing," Cassandra admitted. "Along with working on not blaming myself for what happened, Dr. Fletcher has me trying to live in the minute. And right now I'm going to focus on the fact that I'm fortunate to have a cousin who's my best friend."

Sedona's eyes glistened. "Ditto."

Cassandra blew out a breath. As they shared a hug, she realized how true that was.

"Okay. So, now that we're moving on, I'm going to go book a flight," she said as they separated. "Then pack."

"Will you get mad at me if I say one more thing?" Sedona asked.

"Could I stop you?" Cassandra's smile took the accusation from her tone.

"Probably not," Sedona admitted. "Now that we've gotten my confession out of the way, I just want to state, on the record, that I realize people think I'm crazy to have a spreadsheet for men."

With boxes for the attributes the man that Sedona would accept to settle down with. Cassandra had seen the first sheet, created back when Sedona was still in high school. Over the years, she'd altered the criteria a bit, but the standards had only become more rigid. Perfection was one thing. Perfectionism was, after all, responsible for both her cousin's success as a corporate accountant and her insistence on never scrimping on the very best ingredients that had made her bakery extremely profitable.

But Cassandra had often thought that no mortal man could ever live up to Sedona's exacting standards.

"Not crazy," she hedged now. "Perhaps a bit choosy."

"I've begun to consider that," Sedona surprised her by admitting. "Especially after having become locally infamous for my dates from hell while watching friends find happiness with men I wouldn't have thought they'd connect with...

"But here's the thing...if I ever found a man who obviously loved and cared for me the way Duncan obviously does you, I'd do whatever it took, including moving heaven and earth, to get him back."

Easy for her to say, Cassandra thought. Sometimes love just wasn't enough.

"So." Sedona put her hand on Cassandra's arm. "All I'm asking is that you consider not just the past, which was admittedly problematic, but the future you might be throwing away before you close that final door to your marriage."

"I won't do anything rash." That much Cassandra could agree to, having thought about little else than her and Duncan's marriage over the past months.

"I'm so glad to hear that. You deserve to be happy again." Sedona's dazzling smile could have lit up all of Shelter Bay for a month of rainy coastal Sundays. "Here's hoping that famed Irish magic will spin a reconciliation spell for the two of you."

"I suppose anything's possible."

Because her cousin looked so pleased with that idea, Cassandra opted against revealing that her reason for going to Castlelough was to hand-deliver their divorce papers. Then she was standing over Duncan until he signed on the dotted line.

3

Castlelough, Ireland

OUTSIDE BRENNAN'S MICROBREWERY and Pub, rain was falling from a leaden sky. Inside, a turf fire in a large open hearth warmed against the chill. The whiskey bottles behind the bar gleamed in the glow of brass-hooded lamps; the walls were covered in football flags, vintage signs, and old photographs. The stone floor, Duncan learned as he sat at the bar watching Patrick Brennan pull a row of pints for a group of senior citizens who'd gotten off a Lady sightseeing tour bus, went back to 1650.

"You're very good at that." He'd always believed in giving credit where credit was due, and the publican not only brewed the best beer Duncan had ever tasted, he had an artist's hand when it came to creating a perfect pint.

"I've had enough practice," Patrick said. "And it's important to respect the ale."

"I imagine that's even more the case given that you're the brewer," Duncan said as his phone chirped.

When Diane's photo appeared on the screen, Duncan pressed the button. "Checking up on me to make sure I haven't busted up another tavern?"

The question caused Patrick, who'd returned to the beginning of the row of glasses, to lift a brow. There was an art in pulling pints, and now that the Brian Boru Black Ale had settled, he'd begun topping them off, leaving a creamy crown of froth.

"You may be crazy, but I've never gotten the impression you're suicidal," she responded.

"Tell me you've called with the news that my sentence has been commuted and, as soon as we end this call, I'll be placing another expensive one to Tiffany to buy you a bauble."

"Promises, promises." Her laugh was warm and rich. "And as lovely as that sounds, I might have a problem explaining to my husband why I've let another man, especially one with your dicey reputation, buy me jewelry. So, unfortunately I'll have to turn the enticing suggestion down..."

"No, I'm calling to warn you that Cassandra's on her way to Castlelough."

Emotions too complex to catalog, ones he'd think about later, when he was back in the solitude of Briarwood Cottage, slammed through Duncan like a cluster bomb.

"I suppose that's not surprising," he managed to say even as explosions went off inside his head. "A lake monster is right up her alley these days."

"Beastie," Patrick murmured.

"I don't think the Lady of the Lake is her sole purpose in going." She paused. Duncan tried to remember another time he'd heard his employer's executive assistant so uncomfortable and came up blank. "She asked me where you were staying."

"You're kidding."

"No, I'm not. And promise me you won't yell at me?"

"In all the years you've known me, have I ever yelled at you?"

"No, but you've never exactly been Mr. Rogers, and even less so the past few months... I told her about the cottage."

"Okay." Possibilities began spinning wildly in his head, but Duncan kept his tone neutral. "When is she arriving?"

"She didn't say, but I got the impression that she was going to book a flight out tonight. Which means she'll be at Shannon in the morning."

Duncan had no idea what his estranged wife's intentions might be. The woman who'd been forced through that incredibly painful crucible in Egypt had, understandably, changed. Perhaps she was coming to insist he sign those damn divorce papers she'd sent him. The ones he'd burned in a wastebasket in his Damascus Four Seasons hotel room, setting off the sprinkler system, which had not pleased a staff already tense from the street battles taking place.

Or perhaps she'd tracked him down because having finally overcome her grief, she was ready to move on with her life. He'd kept in touch with her cousin, who, while not at all happy with the idea, had promised to keep their conversations secret. At least for now. But from what Sedona Sullivan had told him, Cass was receiving therapy and had begun to return to the living.

If *that* were the case, the question on the table was whether his wife intended that life to include him.

Damn. Although walking away from their apartment that day had not only ripped his heart to shreds and taken all meaning from his life, Duncan had struggled, against nature, to be patient as her cousin kept counseling restraint.

Now, as thoughts of a possible reconciliation teased seductively in his head, Duncan was relieved, yet again, that Briarwood Cottage was free of the Irish kitsch he'd feared. Thankfully, there wasn't a ceramic leprechaun anywhere in the place. On the contrary, it was a remarkably comfortable two-bedroom home that managed to blend both old and new in perfect harmony. With the view of the lake and castle ruins from the bed, he couldn't have chosen a better location for a reunion. Surely it would remind her of their honeymoon. Of those days and nights when they'd laughed and loved, and the future lay in front of them like a sweet, ripe passion fruit, waiting to be devoured.

Unfortunately, not only did he not have any tropical fruit handy but, except for coffee, his cupboards were bare.

"DOES SHE ENJOY smoked salmon?" Sheila Monohan, of Monohan's Mercantile, asked when a desperate Duncan asked for help planning a late breakfast for his wife.

"Loves it," he said, remembering rare Sunday mornings in New York going out for bagels, cream cheese, and lox, which they'd go home and eat in bed.

"Well, then, you can do a lovely egg scramble with smoked salmon and chives."

"I think I can manage that."

"These brown eggs from Nora Gallagher's laying hens

are wonderful. Nora, of course, was born a Joyce, then she married Conor Fitzpatrick, who was quite the horseman, which, God rest his soul, didn't prevent him from dying in a horrible steeplechase accident." She made a quick sign of the cross without pausing her narrative. "But then, amazingly, given that Castlelough doesn't have many celebrities visiting us here in the back of beyond, she married Quinn Gallagher, whom you may have heard of. He's a famous American writer."

"I've read his books."

"While he's been a very good husband and has done wonderfully generous things for our village, I can't bring myself to read his horror novels," the storekeeper confessed. "There are already so many things to worry about in the world, more every day, it seems; I prefer a nice love story. Though I did read his book about our Lady. It was very well done."

"It was," Duncan agreed. "And one of the few movies that lived up to the book." He didn't mention that the fictional lake creature was what had brought him to town.

"I suspect that's because Quinn was here in Castlelough overseeing every bit of the filming," she suggested. "And staying in the Joyce house, as well, which was how he and Nora met...

"You'll be wanting a selection of scones." She chose three, wrapped them in cellophane, and tossed them in with the salmon and eggs. "As well as our famous brown bread and butter." In went a loaf of bread and a white box of butter bearing what he took to be a family crest depicting two red eagles.

Remembering how Cass had loved the luxury of fresh juice while in the Middle East, Duncan bought Spanish oranges and a juicer.

"The fact that you're going to so much trouble to welcome your wife will make a grand impression," Mrs. Monohan assured him as she rang up his order.

Not nearly as optimistic, Duncan would settle for her not throwing a new set of divorce papers in his face.

Although his career required being able to fall asleep at the drop of a hat, anywhere, anytime, he'd spent a restless night reliving every moment of their time together. *Especially* that last night when she'd coldly, remotely informed him that she no longer loved him and their short-lived marriage was over.

After tossing and turning, he finally gave up on sleep, rose, and set the table with the earthenware dishes he'd found in a cupboard. Reluctantly deciding that meeting Cass at the airport might be pushing things, Duncan brewed himself a big pot of extra-dark roast high-caffeine coffee.

And waited.

4

FROM THE AIR, Ireland looked like an emerald set in a gleaming sapphire sea. As the plane descended into Shannon Airport, Cassandra thought, just as she had the first time she'd been to the country, how all those green fields set apart by stone walls resembled an Irish tourism postcard sprung to life.

Her nerves were tingling as she made her way through immigration. Not because the Irish officials were at all intimidating but because, soon, after these past three months, she'd be coming face-to-face with Duncan again.

Unable to sleep during the flight over the Atlantic, she'd spent the night trying to think of what she'd first say.

"Hi" was way too casual, given their circumstances.

"Hello, Duncan" was better. But then what?

Although they hadn't been able to make their marriage work, he'd done his best to be a caring husband from the moment he'd shown up at the Cairo hospital. Unfortunately, his best hadn't been able to break through the stony wall of Cassandra's grief and guilt. The hard truth was that it had been a losing cause for him to continue to try, which was why, unable to bear his kindness, which, at the time, she'd believed that she hadn't deserved, she'd forced him away.

So, now, months later, she couldn't just hand him the duplicate set of papers she'd had drawn up to replace the ones he'd never signed without some sort of lead-in conversation. What if he slammed the door in her face? She wouldn't blame him. She had, after all, insisted that she no longer loved him.

Which had been a lie. During their third session, Dr. Fletcher had suggested that the person Cassandra had no longer loved was not Duncan but herself. Something Cassandra had been unable to argue with.

Given that Irish road signs could probably earn their own topic on *Jeopardy* (especially those in Gaeltacht regions where they were written in Irish), Cassandra was grateful for the rental car's GPS as she made her way past hedgerows and pastures and through small market towns toward the coast. Rolling down the car windows, she breathed in the salty scent of the sea and the rich, coconut aroma of sunshine-bright yellow furze blooming on hedges, meadows, and along roadsides and felt a light easing of her tangled nerves.

Her first trip to Ireland had been to write about mothers involved in the priest molestation scandal. The last time had been for a delayed honeymoon. Although marriage had never been in her plans, after an AP reporter they'd both known had been killed on the road to Kabul, Duncan had convinced her that since life could often be cut unexpectedly and unfairly short, they should make the most of whatever time they were gifted with.

The very next day, they'd been landing in Barbados where, two hours later, Duncan had slid a slender gold wedding band, bought from the resort's jewelry shop, on her finger. After a single passionate night, assignments had taken them in different directions.

With more than a little string-pulling on both their parts, a month later, they'd managed to meet up again in Dublin while covering an EU economic conference on the collapse of the Celtic Tiger.

Once the conference had wrapped up, after that surfing day in Bonduran, they'd stolen time for a belated honeymoon on Ireland's west coast. It had been in Galway that Duncan had replaced her initial band with a Claddagh ring. The jeweler who'd sold them the matched set had explained that the rings' symbolic two hands holding a crowned heart had been created in the city since the 1700s.

Growing up bouncing back and forth between her globe-trotting parents—who seemed determined to cure all the world's ills through their work with Doctors Without Borders—and life on a commune with Sedona and her parents, then later working in countries where governments and borders seemed in constant flux, Cassandra had appreciated the rings' history and sense of permanence.

After ten days exploring the West from the Ring of Kerry to Galway Bay, most of their last night together had been spent arguing about her destination.

"I'm not some damn submissive Stepford wife who bows to her husband's every demand," she'd insisted as they'd stood on opposite sides of the antique four-poster bed. "I'm an international journalist."

"And a damn good one," he'd shot back. "But you also happen to be my wife, and I don't want to end up a widower before my first damn anniversary."

"But it's all right for me to end up a widow?" she'd

countered, hands on her hips. "Last I looked, Syria is a helluva lot more dangerous than where I'm headed!"

Although they'd argued before (they were, after all, both strong-willed people), that was the first time she'd ever seen his infamous temper in full DEFCON mode.

Finally, as the pink light of dawn was filtering into the cottage, they'd called a truce and managed to make up. In bed.

Later, the drive to Shannon Airport had been mostly silent, as if by unspoken agreement on both their parts not to break the delicate détente. Unfortunately, having left the issue unsettled, once they'd turned in the rental car and made their way to the passenger security checkpoint, the tension swirling between them had become so palpable Cassandra had been relieved when she was finally on the plane leaving the Emerald Isle that had, until that furious fight, been the closest thing to heaven she'd ever known.

A mere three weeks later, while in Egypt to report on women engaged in the democracy movement, she'd gotten swept up in the action, knocked down, trampled, and might have died had it not been for three unknown men who'd lifted her above the crowd and rushed her to an emergency field hospital for wounded protestors.

Where she'd learned that she'd lost the child she hadn't even been aware she'd been carrying.

Within hours Duncan had arrived in Cairo to take her home to the apartment they'd shared on the rare occasion both happened to be in New York City at the same time. He'd stayed for six excruciatingly long weeks, sleeping on the too-short couch so she could have the bedroom to herself, cooking for her, treating her as if she were some fragile piece of his mother's prized crystal collection, about to shatter.

Although Cassandra had still possessed enough pride not to admit it, that was precisely how she'd felt.

During all that time, he'd never once accused her of risking their unborn child's life by putting herself in harm's way. His only mention of her miscarriage was when he'd found her huddled in a tight ball in bed, silently weeping. He'd held her, dried the tears streaming down her cheeks, and assured her that everything would be all right. He loved her and they could have another child.

As if, she'd thought bitterly at the time, children were replaceable, like a camera lens or the aviator sunglasses he was always losing. If Duncan had been anywhere near as heartbroken as she was, he'd certainly kept his emotions well hidden.

Still not having come up with a strategy, she turned down the driveway toward a pretty, whitewashed, thatched-roof house, which a wooden sign proclaimed to be *Briarwood Cottage*. The only rental car available when she'd arrived at the airport was this tiny, two-seater the color of a kiwi. As she pulled up next to the big black Mercedes SUV that Duncan had undoubtedly snagged merely by flashing his killer smile at the tartan-clad woman behind the rental counter, Cassandra felt a stab of something that uncomfortably resembled jealousy.

Damn.

She drew in a deep breath and tried to find her center, as she'd been taught. To focus on the moment.

"Okay," she said, squaring her shoulders as she put the hood up on her jacket and extricated herself from the clown car, "here goes nothing."

5

D URING THE SHORT walk from the car to the cottage, the mist, known locally as Irish sunshine, turned to rain. Cassandra had just lifted her hand to knock on the bright blue door when it opened.

Oh, God. Seeing Duncan again after all this time caused a flutter in her stomach and blurred her brain.

"Cass." His deep voice, known to television viewers all over the world, accelerated her pulse. "You're looking well."

Knowing that jet lag wasn't any woman's friend, Cassandra supposed her appearance was an improvement over those days when her unwashed hair had hung limp over her shoulders and she'd been living in wash-worn pajamas and an oversized plaid robe that she'd bought on a trip to Edinburgh to cover the independence movement.

"Thank you." She cleared her throat. "You, too." Discounting the yellowing around his eye that suggested one of the sailors' fists had connected with his face.

Dressed in a snug black T-shirt and jeans, he looked as hard and fit as he'd been when running around the mountains of Afghanistan, or some jungle chasing down a news story. Or, given the generations of Scots warriors running in his veins, as she'd so often fantasized him—clad in a kilt, fighting off hordes of enemies with a claymore.

A dark stubble roughened his face, and his tousled dark hair looked as if it had been finger combed. When her fingers itched to brush back that lock that always fell over his forehead (and had even been given its own twitter account by news groupie fans), Cassandra realized she'd landed in deep, deep trouble.

Despite her so-called reboot, Cassandra had miscalculated. She wasn't ready for this.

And she so wasn't ready for *him*.

"Why don't you come in out of the rain?" he suggested. His eyes, the warm brown of the whisky his family had first made their fortune brewing, seemed oddly wary. Surely he wasn't as uneasy about this meeting as she was?

The moment she walked across the threshold, Cassandra felt an odd, inner strum, like harp strings being played. While interviewing the mothers of abuse victims, one, a pagan witch from County Kerry, had told her about thin places, also known as places of resurrection, where one's spirit was totally whole, at home, with no longing or yearning to be anywhere else.

Drawn across the room to the window, she looked out onto the view of a crumbling stone castle that had been built on the bank of an impossibly glassy blue lake.

As a frisson of familiarity skimmed up her spine, she belatedly realized Duncan had spoken to her.

"I'm sorry. I was distracted by your view and didn't quite catch what you said." She kept the unsettling sensation that this thatched-roofed cottage might actually be her place of resurrection to herself.

He came and stood beside her, slipping his thumbs into the front pockets of his jeans. "Isn't it spectacular? It's the lake where the Lady supposedly dwells."

She turned her head and looked up at him. He was so close. Too close. All she'd have to do is go up on her toes, just a bit, and their lips would touch and...

No. Don't go there.

"You don't believe in her," Cassandra guessed. He'd always been a realist. Except their first night together, when he'd insisted that they'd been fated to meet. Which, if true, had unfortunately demonstrated that fate had yet other unexpected plans in store for them.

"I believe the town tourism council came up with a clever and apparently successful marketing ploy." He looked down at her, his gaze sweeping over her face. "I asked if you were all right."

"Yes. I am. Mostly." If you didn't factor in the rekindling of emotional ashes she'd thought were cold and safely banked. She took a deep breath. *Center.*

"This is charming," she said, turning toward an arched wall, which opened to a kitchen where a white beadboard ceiling and cabinets brightened the rain-darkened day. Earthenware dishes in varying shades of blue and green echoing the fields and lake outside the windows were stored on open shelves. A rustic wooden farmhouse table had been set for two. "And the name is so evocative. As I drove up, I wondered why we Americans don't name our houses."

When he didn't immediately answer, she shook her head. "Oh, wait. How could I have forgotten? Your family named not only one but two." Although she'd never admit it, there were times when she'd wondered if the reason she'd never met his parents was because he didn't think she'd live up to McCaragh expectations of a daughter-in-law.

"Those names were passed down through the generations with the houses," he said, a bit defensively, reminding her that he'd made a point of telling her that while his parents might take pride in their Main Line Philadelphia "Highlands" and the summer Cape Cod home dubbed "Sea View," he'd always found the names pretentious. "Though you're right about the name fitting this one."

"I especially like the window boxes. The red flowers are so bright against the gray sky… I take it Diane warned you I was coming."

A brow lifted at her abrupt change of subject. "*Warn* might be overstating it. She did call to let me know you'd asked where I was staying, so it was only logical to assume you might be showing up here."

"This isn't exactly your usual five-star accommodation." Cassandra wondered if the cottage had him remembering their honeymoon.

"Far from it. But, as you said, it's charming. And comfortable." If he was thinking of all the hours they'd spent making love in that cloud-soft Irish feather bed, neither his face nor his eyes revealed it. Then again, his career had always depended on his ability to hide his thoughts. "I was also damn lucky to get it. The town's packed with people who've flocked here for the supposed Lady sighting. I suppose that's why you've come?"

"It's what I told my editor."

"Sounds as if it's right up your paper's alley."

"The *Worldwide Buzz* isn't a typical tabloid." And yes,

that was definitely a knee-jerk defensiveness she heard in her voice.

"I figured that out from your Bigfoot story."

"You read it?"

The first story she'd written for the tabloid had been about Sasquatch—who, it turned out, had been secretly heading up a marijuana ring in coastal Washington forests for decades—applying for a business permit to grow and sell pot on the Olympic Peninsula after the state legalized marijuana. Accompanied by expertly Photoshopped pictures of Bigfoot harvesting his plants and cutting the bright yellow Grand Opening ribbon at his Forks, Washington, storefront, the issue had sold out by the second day.

Damn. Cassandra hated the way the idea of Duncan buying the tabloid to read her story caused her heart to do a little cartwheel.

"It was front and center at a newsstand at Kennedy." He dragged a hand through his dark hair, drawing her attention to the woven gold wedding ring he was still wearing. "Damn. I'm forgetting my manners. Let me take your coat so you can sit down and relax after your long flight."

Although she seriously doubted she'd be able to relax anywhere in the proximity of her husband, she shrugged out of the slicker she'd dragged all over the world and handed it to him. The way his eyes darkened to nearly black when their fingers inadvertently touched told Cassandra that she wasn't the only one who'd felt that all-too-familiar electricity spark between them.

He hung the coat on a wooden rack, next to his own, which felt uncomfortably intimate, given their circumstances. Yet also unnervingly right. "Would you like coffee? Or tea? I have regular or a decaf chamomile."

Cassandra definitely didn't need any more caffeine. Needing an energy boost after a sleepless night on the plane, she'd bought an oversized travel cup of triple espresso at the cafe by the arrivals gate as soon as she'd cleared customs. While it *had* managed to keep her awake as she'd struggled with the left-hand driving and roundabouts—which didn't appear to slow down Irish drivers in the least—the high-octane brew had left her feeling even more jangled.

"The chamomile sounds lovely." And hopefully it would calm her nerves, which were jumping around inside her like a toddler who'd scarfed down a giant bag of sugar.

"Tea it is. Have you eaten?"

"I had a muffin at the airport." Which, after her drive from Shannon, seemed like forever ago.

"I thought you might be in the mood for a late breakfast. How does scrambled eggs with smoked salmon sound?"

The sexual awareness between them was gone, replaced by that discomfort she'd sensed when she'd first arrived. Cassandra had been so nervous about this meeting it hadn't occurred to her that Duncan, who'd always possessed enough self-confidence for a dozen lesser men, might also feel uneasy.

"You needn't have gone to any bother."

He shrugged and walked into the kitchen area. "It wasn't any trouble. If I'm going to be stuck here for a month, I was going to have to go shopping someday."

"You were banished for an entire month?" The reports she'd read hadn't mentioned that.

"It was either that or get fired."

"Winston Armstrong would never fire you," she said as she sat down at the table. "He's your godfather."

"Who's never believed in playing favorites. Plus, the way things are going in the news business these days, I wasn't going to take the chance." He took a package of salmon and a blue bowl of eggs out of the fridge. "I'd rather throw myself off that cliff into the Atlantic than take up blogging."

Her answering sputter that neared laughter took her by surprise. Cassandra couldn't remember the last time she'd laughed. Then decided it had been on their honeymoon. Duncan had always been able to make her laugh.

Until he no longer could.

Which hadn't been his fault.

"Given your aversion to settling down, by the third week in even as lovely a place as this, you might find yourself seriously considering taking up cliff diving."

He lifted a brow at her teasing tone, but just then the kettle began whistling, so rather than commenting, he turned away to make her tea. Then placed the pretty green cup on the counter, along with a jar of honey and a bowl of raw sugar.

"You're right. I'd go crazy just sitting around drinking in the scenery," he said. "As it happens, I'm under orders to turn in four stories about the Lady while I'm here."

He cracked the eggs into a mixing bowl, dug out a bit of shell, and began to whisk them with a fork. The scene had her flashing back to those dark days in the apartment, when he'd scrambled eggs, hoping to find something— anything—she'd eat.

"But that's not your kind of story at all."

"Which is exactly what I told Winston." He turned on the flame beneath a black iron skillet and melted a bit of butter the warm color of summer sunshine. There was no butter as rich as Irish butter. While interviewing a woman farmer for her abuse scandal story, Cassandra had learned the flavor came from the local habit of using only summer milk from pastured, grass-fed cows. "I suspect it's his way to teach me a lesson. I also told him—"

She could practically hear Duncan's teeth slam together as he shut his mouth.

"That it was more my type of frivolous tabloid story," she said mildly as she stirred honey into her tea.

"I didn't say that."

"But you were thinking it."

He sighed heavily. "Okay. Yeah. I was. But not in any negative way. It may have been an outlandish concept, but you elevated that story, Cass. Way above tabloid fare. Especially with that bit about Mrs. Sasquatch and their kids being so proud at the ribbon cutting. You actually had me almost believing in, and caring about, the family."

When another silence crashed down between them like a steel wall, she knew he was regretting mentioning children and family. Which was when she belatedly realized that she needed to tell him that he'd done nothing to regret. *She* was the one who bore the burden of guilt. She was the one who'd ruined everything.

Cassandra had thought, after all these months, she had no more tears to shed. Until she felt the sting of moisture behind her eyelids and realized she'd been wrong about this, as well.

Struggling against the all-too-familiar wave of pain, Cassandra took a sip and tasted a blend of apples from the tea and soothing lavender from the honey. "This is excellent."

"I'm happy to hear Mrs. Monohan didn't steer me wrong."

"She definitely didn't. And you don't have to walk on eggshells around me any longer, Duncan. I'm not that same shattered woman you left in Manhattan."

"I didn't want to leave." Was he actually cutting fresh chives? He was.

"I know. Sedona finally told me yesterday." Transfixed by his deft knife skills, despite her best intentions to remain in the moment, Cassandra found herself remembering those dark hands on her body.

"I assume that means she also told you about our conversations."

"She did." They'd always been so wickedly clever, those hands. Always knowing when to draw her into the mists slowly and tenderly or drag her into the fire. Duncan had known Cassandra better than she'd known herself. Which was why, later, she'd been surprised when he didn't realize she was lying to him.

"I knew it was wrong of me to ask her to keep our calls secret, but I didn't feel I had any choice after you sent me away." His tone was heavy with regret, and while he'd always seemed to possess preternatural powers when it came to picking up on vibes, thankfully, he didn't seem to have homed in on her earlier memories of their lovemaking.

"I know now that I must have seemed horribly cruel." If there were awards for understatement, she would've won the grand prize. "And I'm so sorry for that. But at the time, I honestly couldn't be with you." That much was true.

"And now?"

How to safely answer that? When she'd first arrived in Shelter Bay, Cassandra had slept around the clock, rousing only to eat whatever Sedona generously put in front of her. After a few days, she'd moved on to wallowing in cable movies with titles like *The Stranger in My Bed*, *Fatal Vows*, *The Murderer I Married*, and *Death of a Soccer Mom Madam*, in which women got involved with handsome, too-good-to-be-true psychopaths who weren't nearly as charming as they first appeared.

Until she'd eventually moved on from the wife-killer movies to binge watching cooking shows, Cassandra had never given any thought to the idea of cooking being sexy. Now, watching Duncan toss chopped chives into her eggs with one hand while putting brown bread in the toaster with the other had her deciding that he'd be off the meter on any celebrity chef hotness scale.

She shook her head, realizing that he was waiting for an answer. "I came here to see you," she hedged, thinking of those divorce papers in her bag.

"Not the Lady?"

"No. I don't really believe in her, either, though she has the potential to make a great story. But the real reason I came was because we need to talk." And achieve closure to this limbo she'd forced them into.

However, with her body and foggy brain still struggling to catch up to the time change, Cassandra wasn't yet prepared to enter the conversational minefield regarding their divorce. Especially now that parts of her that she'd forgotten even could respond to a hot man were beginning to warm up. Like a torch melting the ice she'd wrapped herself in for so long.

"Well, I'm not going anywhere for the next four weeks. And you're welcome to stay for as long as the cottage is booked, so we've time to deal with the personal stuff…

"Meanwhile, since you've got to be jet-lagged, why don't we stick to easier topics for the time being? Such as how you ended up making such a major career shift."

Once again, he'd read her mind. Hopefully only the jet lag thoughts and not the melting ones. "Do you really care about that?"

"I've always cared about everything to do with you, Cass. From the very first moment. Even with the smoke and the flames and the sirens wailing all around us that day we met, it was as if I was looking through a narrow, close-up lens and all I could see was you."

"Well." She let out a shaky breath. "I don't know what to say to that."

"You don't have to say anything. I decided when Diane called to let me know you were coming that, whatever happens, whatever decision you make, I damn well am not letting go of you, of *us*, without putting my feelings on the table so there'd be no more misunderstandings. Although the concept is scoffed at by most people, I fell in love with you from that first moment I saw you."

"You wanted me."

"Hell, yes. Of course I did. I wanted you then, I wanted you the next morning, I've wanted you every day of my life. I'll *never* stop wanting you.

"But want is easy. And in most cases, fleeting. It's love that made me want to spend the rest of my life with you. Love that makes me ache whenever we're apart. And, in case it's slipped your mind, it's love I pledged that day on the beach. And not just for the easy days, like the last time we were in this country together, but like the words say: for better or worse…

"So." He took a deep, ragged breath. "Now that we've gotten that out in the open for you to think about, why don't you tell me how you ended up the tabloid queen?"

Cassandra was stunned by the intensity of his declaration, which had her remembering in vivid detail how explosive the chemistry had been the moment they'd met. Which undoubtedly had something to do with the fact that he'd been sprawled on top of her at the time while bullets from automatic weapons had been spraying over their heads.

At the time, Cassandra had tried to convince herself that all those sexual vibes zinging back and forth between them had only been natural. Danger was, after all, a proven aphrodisiac.

But rather than diminish, over dinner in Kabul's luxury Serena Hotel's Silk Route Restaurant, the hormone level had soared as hot and high as a comet. Which was how she'd ended up spending that night in his bed.

Unfortunately, like many comets, they'd flamed out and gone crashing back to earth. Which didn't explain the urge to fling herself into his arms.

"I'm far from queen of anything." Was it even possible to have a hot flash at her age?

After a few weeks of therapy and exercise, which involved daily walks on the Shelter Bay beach, she'd felt ready to get back to work but hadn't had the heart to return to writing stories revolving around so much pain and suffering. Which, she'd learned when she'd called editors she'd worked with in the past seeking assignments, was exactly what they expected from her.

"Not surprising, given how hard you'd worked to build your brand," Duncan said when she told him about the less-than-satisfactory conversations. "And burnout is always professional risk. I doubt any serious journalist avoids it forever."

"Even adrenaline junkies?" she asked the man who just happened to be master of that particular universe.

"I suppose that could make the crash even more of a flameout," he suggested in a way that had her wondering which of the two of them Duncan was referring to. Could that bar brawl have been caused by his own personal burnout?

"I suppose it could," she said, deciding he was right about not getting into complex conversational topics while her brain felt as numb as a stone. "I was starting to get discouraged when I received an out-of-the-blue email from Dan Gagnon, an old college friend.

"Dan had carried double majors of finance and journalism because, as much as he enjoyed the fantasy of becoming the next Peter Jennings, he was pragmatic enough to know that he'd never be happy living on a journalist's salary while working his way up a ladder that was losing rungs every day.

"So he spent ten years on Wall Street, cashed in, then bought the *Worldwide Buzz*, which, after a hundred years in business, had sinking revenues and was in danger of going under. Which didn't seem like the wisest financial decision at the time given that tabloids are in as much economic trouble as print newspapers."

Although more recently, the *Buzz* had been kicking

tabloid butt and was even starting to challenge the ubiquitous entertainment magazines.

"They're disappearing like the Tyrannosaurus Rex, because more and more people don't want to read negative stories about their favorite celebrities," she repeated what Dan had told her.

"And with social media being what it is, those who do can read them faster and for free online. Just like the news," he guessed.

"Exactly. If you can count a lot of what's online as *news*," she said. "Anyway, I was curious enough to email him back my phone number, and when he called and told me he wanted me to be his first hire, my first reaction was to refuse."

"Even though you'd already decided that you didn't want to go back to the work you were doing?"

"And wasn't that the dilemma?" she admitted. "I might not want to write about girls getting beaten for wanting to go to school in Afghanistan, but that didn't mean that I wanted to switch to soft, end-of-the-newscast, baby panda stories. Then he explained his plan to take it back to its tabloid roots of 'Gee-Whiz' outlandish stories."

"Like Bigfoot opening up a pot store in a town populated by sparkly vampires."

"Ha!" That drew a full smile, making Cassandra aware of muscles on either side of her lips that hadn't gotten any use these past months. "If you were reading carefully, you'd have noticed that I never once mentioned the vamps. But when many people think of Forks, Washington, that's what comes to mind. Like Astoria, Oregon, and Goonies."

"Or San Francisco and Steve McQueen's car chase."

"Exactly." Oh, God. He still totally got her without her having to explain. That mental shorthand they'd developed made him even more dangerous than the still-smoldering chemistry.

"Anyway, I became more interested when he told me that the main editorial rule would be that the stories should be outrageous. And truth should be avoided at all costs."

"Which actually is a smart move." He plated the eggs and put them on the table. "Because Bigfoot isn't likely to sue anyone for libel anytime soon."

"True enough. The same with the fictional Peruvian archeologist I invented who's supposedly uncovered proof that we're all descended from outer space aliens. People know the stories aren't real life. They read them solely for entertainment value. The same as others might read a novel."

She took a bite of the eggs. "Oh, these are exactly what I wanted. Without knowing I wanted them."

And hadn't he always known exactly what she wanted? What she needed? At least in bed. She hadn't had that many lovers before Duncan, but enough to often feel as if she should have just drawn a map of her body with arrows pointing to the good parts. This man, on the other hand, had proven a master explorer, never missing an erogenous zone. Even ones she'd never known she possessed.

"Remind me to thank Mrs. Monohan the next time I'm in the Mercantile." He put a basket of pastries in the center of the table and sat down across from her, his eyes warming as he returned her smile. It would've been like the old days. If it weren't for the huge pink-polka-dot estranged marriage elephant sucking so much oxygen out of the cottage.

Steeped in her own pain and guilt, Cassandra hadn't probed into Duncan's feelings. One thing she and her husband had in common was that they had both continually put themselves in danger in order to shine a bright light on dark truths. The irony, Dr. Fletcher had helped her see, was that they'd never been courageous enough to shine that same light on the obvious pitfalls in their relationship.

"We're going to have to talk about it, Duncan," she said quietly. Reluctantly.

"I know. But for now, what would you say to just enjoying breakfast? The market didn't have any bagels, but Mrs. Monohan assures me that you can't come to Ireland without sampling the local scones."

He took a raspberry scone from the basket, broke it in half, spooned some cream on it, and held it out to her. As she accepted it from his outstretched hand, Cassandra had a sudden flashback to one honeymoon night when he'd spread rich Irish whipped cream onto her breasts, then licked it off as they rolled over the bed.

A silence settled back over them. One that, while easier than the earlier one, she nevertheless felt the need to fill.

"I may no longer be trying to save the world with my writing, but believe it or not, I enjoy my work."

"I'm glad. You always said you wanted to try fiction."

"Ah, yes." She licked a bit of cream off her thumb, then, as she met his gaze, his darkening eyes told her that they were definitely sharing the same sensual memory. "My novel. The one I'm determined to write so I never have to tell my grandchildren that someday Grandma's going to write a book."

She blew out a long breath. The curtain of silence lowered yet again. When it grew as thick as the fog blowing in from the coast and began to obscure the view, Cassandra decided to try again.

"Speaking of the future—"

"I swear I'm not blowing you off, Cass," he said, his gaze drifting to her mouth for a long, heart-hitching moment before returning to her eyes. "And believe me, I don't like the way we left things so unsettled any more than you do. But you've had a long flight, you've got to be jet-lagged, so since we seem to be managing to get along okay, what would you say to agreeing to a moratorium on the serious stuff for the next couple days?"

The suggestion was undeniably reasonable. Especially since, despite the breakfast, she was starting to crash.

"I suppose that makes sense."

"Terrific." He reached across the table, brushing away a bit of cream from the corner of her lips. It was a good thing she was sitting down, because that light touch had her knees weakening even before he'd licked the sweet cream off his thumb. "You *are* planning to stay here?"

"I was hoping to," she admitted. "Thanks to all the Lady seekers, according to all the hotel and bed and breakfast websites, there's not another room within thirty miles of here." Which, given the narrow hedgerow-lined roads, could take as long as an hour if you got caught in a traffic jam. From past trips to this emerald-green country, Cassandra remembered such jams usually involved a herd of dairy cows or sheep moving pastures. "But now I'm not sure it's such a good idea."

"If you're worried that I'm going to make a move—"

"What was that, with the cream, if it wasn't a move?"

"Okay. You caught me. I plead guilty to an impulsive slip." He lifted his hands and flashed that rogue alpha male smile she'd always suspected had panties dropping all over the globe. "But I promise to be on my best behavior from now on. And you won't have to worry about having to hang a Wall of Jericho between us, because the cottage has two bedrooms."

His reference to the classic Clark Gable, Claudette Colbert's *It Happened One Night*, one of her favorite old movies, was edging toward a move since it brought both their minds back to having watched it—in bed—on their honeymoon when it had shown up on RTÉ.

"Thank you."

Feeling the color rise in her cheeks, she lowered her eyes in an attempt to prevent him from seeing the sensual yearnings that had begun to break through emotional walls she'd spent months building.

6

DESPITE DUNCAN'S WILD, admittedly unrealistic hopes that perhaps Cass had been coming here to initiate a reunion, things were going better than he'd expected. Although it was impossible to ignore the strain hovering in the air like the morning fog blowing in from the sea, they *were* talking. And she was eating the food, which, if he did say so himself, was pretty damn good. Thanks to Mrs. Monohan's excellent advice.

And speaking of good…

The moment he'd opened the door, Duncan had felt his heart stop. Unlike the wounded, ghostlike woman he'd unwillingly left behind, Cass looked good. Better than good. She looked as beautiful as ever. And, thank you, God, healthy.

She'd always been slender, which, he'd realized soon after they'd met during that firefight, was deceptive, because people didn't tend to realize how tough she was. A misconception he'd watched her use to her advantage on more than one occasion.

The world of international journalism wasn't for the weak of heart. It was a tough, balls-to-the-wall, testos-terone-driven environment where women admittedly had to work at least twice as hard as men to be taken seriously. Cass had not only been as tough as any male journalist he'd ever worked with, she was smart as a whip and could hold her own in any situation.

But, as he'd told her during that argument on their honeymoon, that didn't mean that she was bulletproof. Or invincible. Too many journalists had already died covering wars, and new names continued to be added to the glass-walled Journalists Memorial at the national Newseum in Washington, D.C.

Given her toughness, Cass had never been a woman to blush easily. Duncan had always enjoyed being able to bring that soft color into her cheeks.

They'd met during a street firefight in Kabul. When the bullets had started flying, he'd reacted on instinct. After dragging her into a nearby alley behind a pizza joint, he'd pulled her down behind a pile of wooden crates and thrown his body on top of her.

Time had ceased to have meaning. The shooting could've lasted a minute. An hour. An eternity. But when the bullets finally stopped flying and he'd helped her back to her feet, she'd looked up into his face with those lake-blue eyes, and Duncan had known, in that frozen moment in that faraway place, that he was lost.

"You're Duncan McCaragh."

"That would be me," he'd said. "The man who's going to marry you," he'd heard himself saying. "So I suppose, now that the shooting's stopped, it'd be a good time for you to tell me the name of my future children's mother."

She'd both surprised and impressed him by laughing at a time when she would have been forgiven for screaming bloody murder after what they'd been through.

"Sorry, I'm not in the market for a husband."

"Don't worry. I'll change your mind."

She'd laughed again, obviously not taking him seriously. "Give it your best shot."

"I intend to." That had been true then. And was now. "But any good campaign needs proper intel. So, it'd help to know the name of my future wife."

She'd shaken her head in friendly exasperation. "I'm beginning to see why they call you Mad Dog. I can't believe that line actually works. Although I'm too smart to fall for it, I'm Cassandra Carpenter."

He'd recognized her name immediately. "The Cassandra Carpenter who wrote that five-part investigative piece on the murder of the Chinese prostitutes enslaved in Kabul?"

She'd gone undercover as an expat American broker allegedly running an undercover prostitution ring and had later revealed, in vivid, heartbreaking detail, that even in a country as ultraconservative as Afghanistan, sex was for sale. Tragically, at an often deadly price.

"That would be me," she tossed his own words back at him. "The journalist you beat out for the Pulitzer."

"Ouch. I'm sorry about that. But getting grazed by shrapnel undoubtedly won me some sympathy votes that should have gone to you."

"You may have been wounded, which I heard was a lot worse than a 'graze,' but your piece deserved to win without any sympathy votes."

"I like that. It shows that you're not only talented, you have the capacity to forgive." He'd taken hold of her bruised, skinned hand and lifted it to his lips. "Which is even more reason you have to marry me, Cassandra

Carpenter. Because we're a match made in journalist heaven."

Although she'd always insisted that his over-the-top proposal was born solely from the adrenaline rush of their situation, that was another truism that hadn't changed. At least to his mind.

After they'd cleaned up in their individual rooms at the Kabul hotel, he'd taken her to dinner. Before they'd made it to the cheese plate, he'd put the meal on his GNN Platinum card and walked her back to her room, where they'd spent the night heating up the sheets.

From that day forward, Cass had been the only woman for him. Google "animal magnetism" and you'd undoubtedly find their picture. And despite her refusal to admit it after that debacle in Egypt, he'd always be the only man for her.

The challenge, Duncan had decided after hearing that she was on her way to Castlelough, would be to make the most of this serendipitous time together to remind her of what they'd once had. To convince her that while they could never go back to that innocent, sunset time they'd gotten married on a tropical beach, they *could* reclaim their once-in-a-lifetime bond.

One problem was the way they'd parted that morning at Shannon. Which he'd long ago accepted had been his damn fault. His only excuse for acting like an overbearing chauvinist male was the blood-chilling fear of losing her. Too many journalists had already been killed in the Middle East. The possibility of his bride becoming another statistic, one of those tragic fatality stories fellow correspondents would rush to file, had been unthinkable.

Which was why he'd lost his temper when she'd insisted on going to Egypt. A country she'd covered before, and one, as she'd pointed out at the time, that hadn't been as dangerous as the one he'd been headed to. Unfortunately, his bone-chilling fear for her safety had been realized, making it one of the few times in his life Duncan wished to hell he'd been wrong.

When he'd first arrived in Cairo, harried and insane with worry, she'd looked utterly lost. Uncharacteristically vulnerable and tragically broken. But even as he'd sat beside her bed, listening to the doctor relate her various injuries, including the miscarriage, she hadn't wept a single tear. Instead, she'd retreated into a cold, dark place, and nothing he'd attempted over the next six weeks together back in New York had managed to infiltrate it.

He'd always known what Cass was thinking. Or feeling. They'd been synced in a way Duncan had never felt with any other person. Enough so that he'd been naive, or arrogant, enough to believe the connection between them would be impossible to sever.

But he'd been wrong. Once they'd returned home to the States, he'd felt totally incapable of knowing what was going through that talented mind. Or how to reach her wounded, ice-encased heart.

When she'd told him that she no longer loved him and sent him away, she'd driven a stake through his heart. But even that hadn't made him fall out of love with her. She might as well have tried to force the sun to stop rising in the morning. Or setting in the evening.

The thing to do, Duncan decided now, was to channel his inner Marine. Winning Cassandra Carpenter back was the most important mission he'd ever embark on.

And just like those other missions, failure was not an

option.

Meanwhile, understanding she needed some time and space to adjust, he decided to write those damn stories for Winston. Because while there was nothing the billionaire network news titan couldn't buy for himself, Duncan definitely owed him for sending him to Ireland.

7

WELL. THIS CERTAINLY wasn't what she'd expected. Not that she'd known what to expect, which had been part of Cassandra's problem. Unlike her überplanner, perfectionist cousin, a life bouncing back and forth between traveling the globe with her parents and staying on the commune with Sedona—whenever her mother and father took off for somewhere they felt was too dangerous for their daughter—had taught Cassandra to not only accept the unexpected but to thrive on it.

Until Egypt.

On their wedding day, as the sun had set into the sea in a dazzling red glow, Cassandra had realized that her entire life had become divided into *Before Duncan* and *After Duncan*.

Until that tumultuous, terrifying day when she'd lost that child she'd never gotten to share with her husband had taken over the top place.

But what, she wondered, as she watched Duncan put the plates into the dishwasher, if it might be possible to recapture what they'd had together? He'd always been an expert at hiding his thoughts, but unless she was totally misreading him, which could be possible since she wasn't as sure of anything as she'd once been, he was pleased she'd shown up here.

After all, he'd gone to the trouble of shopping at the local store, asking the shopkeeper for menu advice, actually giving thought to a meal instead of dialing for takeout as they usually did on those rare occasions when they were together in New York.

Of course, the main reason for all that takeout Chinese and pizza was because they'd spent so much stolen time together making love.

Which hadn't left much time for talking.

It occurred to her now that she knew little about her husband other than he came from old financial wealth, had dropped out of Princeton, and that his mother was a "functioning" alcoholic. She'd figured out for herself that he wasn't close to his family when, months after their wedding, he was still dodging her questions about when she was going to meet James and Angela McCaragh.

Cassandra had spoken briefly with them on the phone the day after the wedding. James's cool, patrician tone hadn't invited familiarity, while Duncan's mother, who, only a bit warmer, had informed Cassandra that she hoped for grandchildren.

Something that definitely hadn't been in their plans. At least not in the near future. After all, it would have been impossible to care for a family while they were both chasing to all corners of the globe at a moment's notice.

After Cassandra returned to New York from Egypt, Angela had called again late one night, but apparently the "functional" part of Duncan's mother's drinking problem hadn't been in full operational mode. After five minutes of listening in on the painful rambling, Duncan had taken the phone away from Cassandra, calmly informed his mother they appreciated her call, and hung up.

And that had been that.

Despite everything she'd witnessed as a correspondent, Cassandra was, at heart, an optimist. She might have lost the ability to hope and dream, but there were more and more times, like now, when she could feel a flicker of spirit that had managed to survive.

After Egypt, she'd been so badly broken she hadn't been certain that she'd ever be able to put herself back together again. But she had and she was growing stronger every day. Three months ago, she hadn't even been able to leave Sedona's apartment. Two months ago, she wouldn't have thought she'd ever get back on a plane. Especially by herself. But she had gotten on that plane and come here today, divorce papers in hand, certain that her marriage was irrevocably broken.

Now, after his unexpected declaration, she was confused. And conflicted.

"Why don't you take a nap?" Duncan suggested as her eyelids grew heavy. "Then later, maybe if you feel up to it, since scrambled eggs is pretty much the height of my culinary expertise, we can drive into town and get a late lunch or early supper at the pub."

"As lovely as breakfast was, I am capable of feeding myself," she said, not wanting him to think that just because the spark was still there between them she was going to leap into the flames.

"Of course you are. But you have to eat. And I have to eat. And if you could see the contents of my refrigerator, you'd understand why I'm suggesting letting someone else do the cooking."

She could go to the market herself tomorrow, Cassandra decided. Meanwhile, with more important issues to deal with, this was not a hill to die on. Except...

Having dinner with Sedona and her friends in a familiar place was one thing. Going out in public with a man who drew attention wherever he went was a challenge she wasn't sure she was prepared for.

"While you're catching up on sleep, I'll go track down something resembling a story for Winston," Duncan suggested as her weary mind debated with her heart. "We can talk about what to do for dinner when I get back."

As he carried her bags down the short hallway to the bedroom, Cassandra decided that as much as she wanted—needed—to settle matters, waiting until she was better-rested made sense.

After all, not only was Duncan stuck here for a month, she could work from anywhere, and it wasn't as if she had a hard deadline. Dan Gagnon had been more than willing to take her stories whenever she turned them in.

The bedroom was as charming as the rooms she'd seen thus far. The interior stone walls had been painted white, the floor lake-blue. A black iron bed echoed the simple black frames of the photographs of local landscapes and children adorning the walls. A blue and white quilt on the bed had been turned down to reveal white sheets.

After stripping off her travel-rumpled clothing, Cassandra slid between those sheets that carried the clean, fresh scent of line drying she remembered all too well from their honeymoon, then fell like a stone into sleep.

8

U NREASONABLY DISTRACTED BY his wife sleeping—alone—just down the hallway, Duncan headed into town to see what he could discover about the mythical Lady. Deciding that few would know what was going on in the town better than a bartender, he dropped back into the pub.

"So, has anyone in this town actually ever seen the Lady?" he asked Patrick Brennan, who was back behind his bar.

"I personally only know the stories second-and third-hand," Patrick said. "But there are those who have more familiarity with the subject."

"I don't suppose you'd be willing to share names?"

"As it happens, I suspect Patrick would be referring to me," a man sitting next to him at the bar commented. He held out a hand. "Michael Joyce. I've been looking forward to meeting you."

The name was instantaneously recognizable. Duncan narrowed his eyes and studied the man dressed in jeans, work boots, and a black fisherman's sweater more closely. His hair was shot with strands of silver, and his features were more chiseled than the ones on the back of his award-winning books, but it was a face that Duncan knew well.

"Word gets around fast."

"It does, indeed," Patrick said as he dipped a pint glass into some sudsy water in the sink behind the bar. "Though, in this case, it's not so much local gossip as for the fact that you happen to be speaking with your landlord."

Okay. That was unexpected. "*You* own Briarwood Cottage?"

"That and a few others," Michael Joyce said as he lowered a heavy mug of coffee to the bar. "As much as I enjoy farming, during the winter months when the land lies fallow, I found myself getting restive. So, I began restoring—"

"More like rebuilding from a rubble pile," Patrick Brennan interjected.

"I was fortunate to have your brother doing most of the building while I served as a laborer," Michael responded to Patrick. "Bram's more than just a contractor. The way he can re-envision a famine cottage, keeping the historical bones while making it livable again, reminds me of those cathedral builders of old."

"Don't be telling him that," Patrick said. "He can be insufferable enough to live with."

The laugh they shared suggested a long and close friendship. A revolving door of first boarding schools and later Duncan's vagabond life had precluded such relationships. There were many other reporters he was friendly with, but none he could actually call friends. He'd always been a loner.

Until Cass. Who'd been not only the woman he loved

but his one true friend. Which was why, on the anniversary of their meeting this week, he'd admittedly gone off the rails and ended up in that brawl. Yet, showing the serendipitous nature of life, hadn't that tumble brought him here to Ireland? Even if he'd searched the entire world, he couldn't have found a better location to remind his wife of the connection they'd once shared.

"I'm impressed," he said, returning to the conversation. "It's obviously not new construction, but no way would I have guessed that it dates back to the 1800s."

"It does indeed," Joyce said. "That cottage, like Fair Haven, which was the first I restored, once belonged to my family. As did the castle, in ancient times. Though it's true enough that some of the famine homes Bram and I have been salvaging were little more than ruins from a tragic time."

"When their occupants left either on death carts to be put in the ground or coffin ships across the Atlantic to Canada and America," Patrick said.

"Or Australia, often for the so-called crime of stealing a loaf of bread or rasher of bacon to feed a starving family." An apple-cheeked man who brought to mind an ancient leprechaun sitting on the other side of Joyce joined the conversation. From his sour tone, he could have been talking about an event that had occurred yesterday, which wasn't all that surprising, since Duncan had discovered early in his career that displaced populations tended to have very long memories.

"There are also those who'd be telling you that many of the residents never entirely left," the elderly man added. "That the cottages would be haunted."

"I'm not going to be one to discount the possibility

that, given their former circumstances, some spirits would have found moving on a bit challenging," Michael Joyce allowed. "But I've yet to hear a complaint, so if there were to be any ghosts hanging around, they're benevolent ones who aren't into disturbing the guests."

"The woman who booked the cottage didn't mention your being the owner." Duncan would've been a great deal more eager about this trip had he known he'd be meeting a man he'd admired for so many years.

"That's because all bookings are done anonymously through a property leasing agent," the old man piped up again before Joyce could answer. "Our Michael is one who enjoys his privacy. Why, when he first arrived back in Castlelough, didn't he act like an old hermit monk, living out there all alone on his farm? Then his daughter appeared out of the blue from the North and—"

"That would be a story for another time, Fergus," Joyce said firmly.

Duncan didn't need his journalism instincts to realize that the topic of Michael Joyce's daughter, whatever its nature, was a sensitive one.

"I've studied all your books," he said, returning the conversation to its original track in order to fill in the silence that had fallen. "Especially those from your war photojournalism days."

Joyce had reportedly died, he remembered, on the helicopter lifting him out of a marketplace massacre in Kosovo. After being brought back to life, he had seemed to disappear for a time. Until reinventing his career with photography books showcasing such topics as the courage of hospitalized children, daily life in the Irish West, and another, more recent one that followed the nomadic lives of Irish travelers.

"I'm more a television correspondent than a photographer," Duncan said, "but there have been times in wars zones when I've been forced to resort to taking video with my cell phone, and while it's a different medium, your work, the way you always knew how to capture the money shot that told the story, was like learning from a master."

"It's glad I am that my work proved helpful," Joyce said mildly. "And I certainly tossed enough that never worked out... But that was another lifetime. Now I'm merely a family man, a farmer, a restorer of crumbling buildings, and an occasional photographer when the muse deigns to visit.

"And speaking of visits, I hope your romantic breakfast with your wife went well."

Duncan wasn't surprised, given his so-called celebrity and the size of the town, that his shopping expedition had already become news. "I don't remember saying anything to Mrs. Monohan about romance."

"While I may have been out of journalism for several years, I'm Irish enough to recognize an intriguing story when I hear one. It's only a shame all the Lady seekers are in town, or you and your wife could have a picnic on the shores of Lough Caislean. The castle ruins are spectacular at sunset. It's also when our beastie is most likely to appear."

"Are you saying you believe in her?"

"I, myself, have always been agnostic on the topic. But I personally know some who do believe."

"I don't suppose you'd be willing to share names."

"To a reporter?" Joyce shook his dark head and took another longer, considering drink of coffee. "No, although you seem like a good enough fellow, it's not my story to tell. Nor my place to reveal a confidence."

Duncan heard the finality in the former war photojournalist's tone and knew he'd run into a dead end. Which only meant he'd have to find another source.

"Though I can speak with someone," Joyce offered after a pause. "To see if he'd be willing to share his tale. If so, I'll have him ring you."

"I'd appreciate that." Duncan dug into his pocket and pulled out a card. "Here's my number."

"I wouldn't be holding your breath," Joyce warned. "And because I'm personally very fond of him, I'd be needing your word that you wouldn't be about making him look like one of those sad lunatics who wear tin foil hats and fret about space aliens landing in Castlelough. He's most definitely sane and highly intelligent."

"You have my word," Duncan promised.

Michael Joyce gave him a long look that reminded Duncan that this was a man who was alive after years of living and working in war zones because he'd learned to see beyond the surface. As Duncan himself had.

"He's in Galway at the moment. But he'll be here tomorrow morning visiting family. I'll talk with him then, and if he agrees, he can ring you. If he's not interested in being part of your story, I'll call you myself."

"I can't ask for any more than that."

"Then it's done." He polished off the coffee and tossed a bill onto the bar. "Have a grand day." He was nearly to the door when he turned back. "We'll be having a *seisiún* here tonight with a few of the locals if you think your wife would enjoy a bit of *craic*."

"I'll ask her." Truthfully, after the way she hadn't

jumped at his suggestion earlier, Duncan had no idea if Cass would be up for a traditional Irish music session. But if she happened to enjoy herself, he'd have a better chance of delaying any divorce talk for at least one night.

"After her long trip, it may take her a while to get up to speed," Patrick Brennan said. "Why don't I put your name on a snug? We've a fine one in the back that offers more privacy than those up here in front."

"I'd appreciate that."

The snug went back to those days when not everyone would want to be seen in a pub. Mostly having been originally frequented by ladies who weren't allowed to drink in a bar, or a garda at the end of his policing rounds, a priest having his nightly whiskey before turning into bed, or lovers engaged in a clandestine rendezvous, they were also popular as a safe place for young children to sleep while their parents enjoyed the music and dancing. Once entirely private, the glass doors in Brennan's allowed patrons to be seen while also providing a place for a private conversation.

Having achieved some measure of success, what with a possible source to interview tomorrow, as much as he wanted to return to the cottage and crawl between those fragrant white sheets with Cass, Duncan left the pub and went to Monohan's again. After assuring the helpful storekeeper that his wife definitely enjoyed her breakfast, he bought crackers, cheese from Michael Joyce's farm, and wine for a pre-supper snack. Along with a box of spaghetti and a jar of imported Marsala sauce in the more likely event they'd be staying home.

Home. Although he'd been a rolling stone most of his life, once he'd met Cass, Duncan had begun entertaining thoughts of settling. Thoughts he'd kept to himself, because given her energy, which could make the Energizer Bunny look like a tortoise, he hadn't gotten any impression that she'd been ready to set up housekeeping.

Yet, the moment she'd walked into Briarwood Cottage this morning, something had clicked. Something that had him thinking that perhaps that incident in the bar had been a wake-up call that a flameout was on a not very distant horizon.

As he'd scrambled those eggs, he'd thought how much pleasure there was in what was, to most people, an ordinary domestic task. The idea of eating breakfast with Cass every morning, after sleeping in the same bed with her at night, was more than a little appealing.

And although he was wary about getting his hopes up too high, the thought of starting a family admittedly added to that appeal.

Once they'd returned to New York from Egypt, Duncan had gone with Cass to all her doctor appointments. As a reporter, he'd always been single-minded in uncovering the story. The reasons why something happened. Or, as they'd taught in journalism class, the *Who, What, When, Where, Why,* and *How* of an event.

The thing about miscarriages, he'd learned, was that while the best doctors in the world might know those first four facts, those all-important fifth and six facts remained a mystery.

In Cass's case, her injuries pointed to the most logical cause. However, the doctor had told her, her miscarriage could well have happened at any time. There was, they were told, often no rhyme nor reason.

As much as he'd grieved the loss of their child, what

had been more heartbreaking was Cass believing he might think she'd purposely kept her pregnancy a secret so he wouldn't try even harder to prevent her from going to Egypt.

He'd admittedly been sick with worry, but not for one instant when the Cairo GNN bureau chief had called him with the news had that suspicion even crossed his mind.

The doctor had gone on to explain that many women miscarry before they know they're pregnant. That often what they mistake for a period is actually abnormal break-through bleeding.

Which must have happened with Cass, because she'd been ten weeks pregnant when she'd miscarried. Although they hadn't learned the baby's sex, Duncan would always privately believe she'd been a girl. With her mother's expressive lake-blue eyes and hair the warm, golden color of honey. In his mind, he'd named her Skye. For his family's ancestral lands and the warm, happy color of a sunlit summer day.

Because Cass had been so wounded, no, so *shattered*, he'd grieved in silence, trying to care for her. To support and comfort.

But he'd failed. And in doing so, had lost not only a child but the wife he loved beyond reason, as well.

But that was then. And this was now. And Cass was not only in Ireland, she was in his cottage.

Which was, Duncan thought as he headed back to Briarwood Cottage after some less-than-successful conversations with locals about the Lady, a start.

9

CASSANDRA AWOKE TO find the cottage quiet. The only sound was the patter of a light rain on the roof. She called out, and when there was no answer, she decided Duncan must still be out digging up a story about the Lady seekers.

At least she hoped that was what he was doing. She hadn't come all this way to end up bailing him out of Castlelough's jail for pub brawling.

The little antique clock on the bedside table revealed that she'd been sleeping for three hours. Which at least partly made up for the sleepless night she'd spent trying to decide what to say to Duncan.

Despite the long nap, her head still felt fuzzy and a bit floaty. She was also stiff from long hours sitting crowded between two businessmen, both of whom had commandeered the armrests and the overhead bin, leaving her squeezed into the compact middle seat like a sardine packed into a can. Deciding to take a walk to explore her surroundings and work out the kinks, she wrote a note to Duncan, which she left on the kitchen table, put on her coat and a wool hat she'd bought in a Shelter Bay dress shop, and left the cottage.

A rainbow arched across a rain-washed sky the color of the inside of an oyster shell and over stone walls studded with shamrocks and moss. Except for the rustling of leaves in the trees and the musical trill of hidden songbirds, Cassandra found herself surrounded by absolute stillness.

In the distance, framed by the shimmering rainbow, the lake shone like polished silver. Surprisingly, none of the Lady seekers she'd seen crowding the streets of Castlelough as she'd driven through the village had made their way to the reedy banks. Or even to the hills, topped by the crumbling castle ruins that, along with the lake, had given the town its name.

She was wondering about that as she passed a cemetery, a somber place of high Celtic crosses standing like silent sentinels. A few rounded gravestones, names worn away by salt winds and the ages, were covered with pale green moss. She was able to make out several Joyce family names among the stones.

She continued on, over ancient mountains crumbling their way to dust, pausing at a mound of earth blanketed with flowers and decorated with stones. Cassandra had read about cairns, burial chambers that archeologists dated to five thousand years in the past, but standing beside this one, she could almost imagine the voices of those who'd crossed through the thin curtain between realms.

And although it was undoubtedly only a figment of her imagination, stirred by being in such an evocative place, she thought she'd heard some of them whispering her name as she walked away.

After turning a corner, she came to a towering hedge ablaze with shockingly pink fuchsia entwined with white flowers attached to thorny limbs guaranteed to keep trespassers outside. Still, she considered as the impenetrable-appearing greenery stretched for as far as the eye could see, she would have expected at least a few of the more ardent Lady seekers to have shown up with hedge clippers in hand.

Dragonflies flittered around the bushes, performing aerial ballets as they spun and turned, their bodies gleaming like jewels, their wings a sparkling and iridescent translucence in the shuttering rays of the sun breaking through the clouds. The buzzing drone of fat bees flying from flower to flower added deep base notes to the high treble whirr of the dragonflies' wings.

Cassandra remembered an elderly woman at the commune, who, along with making honey for the members to sell at local farmers' markets, had supplemented her living by performing psychic readings at the markets, fairs, and to private clients who, from the luxury cars that would show up from time to time, profited quite well from her advice.

One summer, when the skies were filled with dragonflies, she'd told Cassandra and Sedona that they represented change, not just in one's life but in emotional growth and self-realization.

The ever-pragmatic Sedona had scoffed at the woman's pronouncement that the dragonfly's skittering flight across water represented the act of looking beneath the surface, into the deep implications of life.

"If they represent looking deeper, why do they fly so fast over the water?" she'd asked.

The fortune-teller, apparently not used to being challenged, had gathered up her crystal ball and tarot cards and gone marching back to her small, brightly painted house, colorful skirts swaying.

"I hope she doesn't put a curse on us," Cassandra had said, only partly kidding.

Her cousin had merely shrugged. Even at thirteen, she'd been the most sensible, down-to-earth person Cassandra had ever met. "Zelda's always been thin-skinned. It was a logical enough question."

Which had been true enough. But when Cassandra's parents had died in that earthquake two weeks later, she couldn't help wondering.

Unable to go any farther, she made her way back down the trail to the cottage, only to find that Duncan still hadn't returned. Which, even though she knew she should be relieved, left her feeling more than a little disappointed.

Despite the sun struggling to shine, she felt damp and chilled from her walk. Retrieving her shampoo and body soap from her carry-on, she went into the bathroom located in the hallway between the bedrooms and was surprised to find it spotless.

The Duncan she remembered hadn't bothered to unpack, and since hotel rooms came with maids—who were admittedly tipped well—housekeeping had never been a priority. Then again, she thought as she stripped off the underwear she'd been sleeping in, she'd never known him to cook, either. Apparently she hadn't been the only one who'd changed over these past months apart.

The warm shower water sluicing over her felt like nirvana. Tilting her head back, she closed her eyes and felt it washing away the travel grunge, along with lingering fatigue and tension.

The problem was that, like everything else about Briarwood Cottage, it brought back memories of their Irish honeymoon and the way Duncan had stripped her out of her clothes that had gotten soaked on a visit to the Cliffs of Moher, shed his own, then pulled her into the shower, where their lovemaking had definitely steamed up the bathroom more than the hot water.

She could have stayed there forever, had it not been for the limits of the cottage's water heater. Lost in sensual memories, which had morphed into fantasies of Duncan spreading soapsuds all over her body, Cassandra hadn't noticed the loss of water temperature until she was suddenly shocked back to reality.

She yelped and leaped out from beneath the now-icy water. Making matters worse, as she stood shivering and dripping on the soft white rug, she realized that she'd forgotten to bring in a change of clothing. After quickly drying off, she wrapped a thick towel around her freezing body and made a dash for the bedroom.

Just as Duncan appeared in the hallway.

10

"SORRY," HE SAID as she froze like the proverbial deer in the headlights. "I assumed you'd still be sleeping."

"I woke up a bit ago." She tugged the towel up a few inches. Duncan supposed that if he were a gentleman, he'd turn away, but hell, drinking in the sight of her creamy shoulders and long, bare legs, he told himself it wasn't as if she were a stranger.

Didn't a husband have some right to enjoy looking at his wife?

"I was taking a shower," she said. "I'm afraid I used up all the hot water."

"No problem." He gave her his best smile. The same I'm-harmless-and-want-to-be-your-friend smile he'd pull out when interviewing locals in terrorist territories. "How are you feeling?"

"Better." She managed a faint return smile even as she held the towel so tight her knuckles were turning white. "That bed's like sleeping on a cloud."

"It's the goose down," he said. "Like what we had in the other cottage. The bed in the other room is the same."

Although much lonelier than their honeymoon one.

"I hope you slept well."

"I did. I also took a walk."

"In the rain?"

"I don't melt. And it was mostly just mist by the time I woke up. I went a little past the cemetery. And the cairn."

"I checked that shortly after I arrived. I've never been one to believe in ghosts, but there's definitely something, like lingering spirits, going on there."

"Like what they say about the veil being thinner," she agreed. "I felt it, too. Like ghosts standing guard over the past."

"Exactly."

"Well…" She went to drag a hand through her wet hair, causing the white towel to slip a bit. Duncan wouldn't lie—he wouldn't mind if it dropped to the floor. "I suppose I'd better get dressed."

"I'll put the groceries away," he said. "I was going to make coffee. Would you like some? Or tea again?"

"Coffee would be great."

"Got it."

They stood there, him looking down at Cass, her looking back up at him. Although they were a few feet apart, he could almost feel the cord connecting them and wondered if she felt it as well.

"I'm dripping on your floor." Yet she didn't move.

"It's Ireland. I'd bet the floor can handle it." Because she still hadn't run away, he indulged in taking her in, from the top of that unfamiliar short hair down to her bare, nude toes, which had always been tipped in bright colors.

Since their work hadn't taken them to places where mani/pedis were easily available, she'd colored them herself. Just thinking of watching her, brow furrowed in deep concentration as she painted them a deep, tropical coral while rockets exploded over their hotel, was enough to make him semi-hard. Although she'd complained the next morning about him having smudged the polish, she'd laughed as he'd half carried, half dragged her the few feet to the bed.

"You've always looked good wet," he said.

She tilted her chin up in a pissed-off way that was all too familiar. And welcome. He'd been at a total loss on how to deal with the wounded sparrow he'd found in that chaotic, makeshift Egyptian clinic that could have been one of the lower rings of hell.

"If I were keeping track, I'd say that was another move."

"Ah, but if it were, and I'm not saying it was, perhaps I was encouraged by my wife greeting me home in nothing but a towel."

This time her color was born from a quick flash of temper, which, perversely, he was happy to see. "You're as incorrigible as ever."

"And you're as beautiful as ever."

She shook her head and blew out a breath. "I'm going to get dressed." She turned on her heel and marched back toward the guest bedroom.

The Emerald Isle might be world-famous for its scenery, but as far as Duncan was concerned, Cass's very fine butt walking away equaled any view the country offered.

She firmly closed the door between them. It wasn't exactly a slam, but close.

Another encouraging step forward, he decided as he strolled into the kitchen to start the coffee. An annoyed wife was not an indifferent one.

11

HAVING BEEN PREPARED to heat up the jar of spaghetti sauce, Duncan was surprised when Cass came out of the bedroom, dressed in a snug blue sweater dress a few shades darker than her eyes and a pair of short, red, pointed-toe cowboy boots she'd picked up on Mulberry Street during one of their rare times together in New York.

He hadn't lied when he told her she looked lovely. She might not be all the way back, but her new shorter hair enhanced her expressive face, the lost look was no longer in eyes as blue as Lough Caislean, and her smile, while not yet as dazzling as he knew it could be, still warmed the gray Irish evening.

"Thank you," he said.

"For what?"

"For wearing that dress."

"It's new." Appearing a bit nervous, she ran her hands down her sides. "Sedona dragged me out shopping at this little Shelter Bay boutique last week."

"I'll have to remember to thank her, too."

The dress hugged her body in a way that had his fingers perversely itching to peel it off her. Beginning at the hem, which ended mid-thigh, then up over her sweet spot, where he'd linger just long enough to make her as crazy as being anywhere near her was making him, then higher, to breasts with nipples he knew to be the color of a deep pink rose.

And, damn, if he kept thinking like this, he was going to walk into the pub with the mother of all boners. And wouldn't that provide some fun entertainment for the locals?

"I've always liked those boots," he said, trying to take his mind away from doing her right here on the couch. Now. Unfortunately, thinking about the boots didn't work either as he remembered telling her in the store that she'd looked hotter than a firecracker in them. Which was exactly what she'd been a few hours later, after they'd returned to their apartment. "That was a good day."

After she'd tried on at least a bazillion pairs of boots, they'd wandered into a nearby Little Italy restaurant where they'd shared a bottle of red wine and an ultra-thin-crust pepperoni pizza smothered in mozzarella and a rich red sauce that would have made any Italian nonna proud.

"Any day not dodging bullets is a good day," Cass agreed as she sat down on the sofa beside him. "I'm sorry about whatever happened in that bar that got you banished to here," she said as they took in the view of the hills, the castle, and the lake.

He lifted his shoulders in a shrug. "I'm no longer considering this trip a banishment, thanks to you showing up. Though that wasn't my best moment," he admitted, wondering if this week was equally difficult for her. Or had she put the anniversary of their meeting and the first time they'd made love away the same as she'd put him away?

"I started writing about it on the flight here," she surprised him by admitting.

"You were writing about me?"

"Not you. I don't write about real people anymore, remember? No, I used Fleet Week and the idea of the Lady as inspiration for a piece about some ancient sea serpent stowing away on a Navy cruiser as it crossed over the Bermuda Triangle."

"Bermuda Triangle myths probably are popular in your business." Duncan wasn't as surprised as he'd once been at her career change.

"People eat them up," she agreed. "Along with extra-terrestrials, UFOs, and anything to do with the Titanic or Section 51."

"I liked that one you wrote last week about the Titanic survivor being rescued from a melting glacier after having been raised by polar bears."

She angled her head and studied him. "You really *have* been reading my stories."

"You've always had a remarkably engaging writing voice. Fiction, even if it's labeled as tabloid fiction, has given your imagination free rein. As outlandish as that one was, I immediately saw how it could easily be slanted into an allegorical novel about an outsider suddenly having to find the skills to fit into a society that doesn't really have a place for him."

"That was how I first conceived it," she admitted. "Because once I stopped racing around the world, I realized that perhaps I'd been so caught up in chasing stories about other people's lives, I'd never allowed myself to slow down enough to think about my own life. Where I fit in."

"I'm not sure people like you and I *do* fit in all that well." Duncan had been giving that matter more than a little thought himself. "Neither of us had much stability growing up, between your bouncing back and forth between living with your parents and with your cousin's family and me being sent off to all those boarding schools.

"Then, while we might have been to more locations on the planet than most people, because of what we were covering, our world became more and more narrowed down to the dark places. It's not as if details surrounding the most recent genocide make for engaging dinner party conversation."

"I haven't been to any party, let alone a cocktail party, for longer than I can remember."

"We could remedy that," he suggested. "I was told they're having a *seisiún* at the pub this evening."

"Oh." The light that had brightened her face while they'd been talking about her work seemed to fade. Like a candle being snuffed out. She dragged a hand through her hair, which had begun to curl as it dried, again. "While dinner sounded nice enough, I'm not sure I'm really up to all that."

"Understandable, given that it's your first day here. And Patrick Brennan, the owner, realized that when he invited us. He said there's a more private snug in the back he can save for us."

"If I say yes to that, are you going to talk dirty to me?"

"Only if you want me to." Her question brought back that pub grub supper they'd eaten in a snug during their honeymoon. It had been after he'd bought them the matching rings. "And, for the record, I wasn't talking dirty that night in Galway. I was merely telling my wife all the things I wanted to do to her. And have her do to me...with me."

The color streamed back, like a brilliant sunrise lighting her from the inside out. "This isn't going to work."

She wasn't talking about eating dinner, and they both knew it. "We'll never know if we don't give it a try," Duncan coaxed. "I'm not asking for a lifetime commitment, Cass." As far as Duncan was concerned, she'd already agreed to that. He'd just have to make her realize that some things, some people, were worth fighting for. "Just a friendly night out. And if you're worried about me jumping you—"

"Since you set the bar for honesty earlier, I'll have to admit that I'm concerned about just the opposite. About me jumping you."

Score one for his side. "And that would be a bad thing why?"

"Because it would just complicate our situation even more."

"You said the same thing the morning after our first dinner at the Serene," he reminded her. "About how you didn't have the time or place in your life for complications."

"It wasn't *dinner* that made things complicated. It was spending the night together," she corrected. "And look how that turned out."

"It wasn't all bad," he reminded her. "We might not have had Paris, like Rick and Ilsa before they met up again at Rick's Place in Casablanca. But we *did* have Barbados and Ireland."

"Which adds up to all of ten days and one tropical

night."

"It could have been more if our lives hadn't been taken out of our hands." He paused. Then went for broke. "Maybe it's time we finally took them back."

That stopped her.

"Do you really believe that's possible?"

Failure was not an option. "We'll never know if we don't try… Remember what you said when you caved in and agreed to marry me?"

"That it was madness and we'd be insane to even try to make a marriage work."

"After that. While we were on the beach, right before we exchanged vows. That you'd rather—"

"Regret making a mistake than look back and regret not having taken the risk," she said. Cassandra blew out a breath. Closed her eyes briefly, then, as her stomach growled, shook her head.

"I'm only giving in when it comes to dinner," she warned as she stood up.

"I'll take that," Duncan agreed.

It was, he reminded himself again, a start.

12

FIVE MINUTES LATER, they were driving down the narrow, winding road that occasionally offered glimpses of the cliffs and sea beyond before turning back to hug the heather-studded mountain. The rain had begun again, and for the first few minutes, there was only the hiss of water beneath the tires and the swish, swish, swish of the wipers sweeping the water off the SUV's windshield.

"So, did you get your story?" Cass asked as Duncan braked for some sheep being herded across the road by a thick-coated dog. The sheep's backs had been spray-painted a bright, fluorescent green to mark ownership.

"The beginnings of one," he said. "There seemed to be more people here looking to win the photo lottery with a picture of the creature than there are ones who actually believe in her."

"Did you talk to the townspeople?"

"I tried. But although they were friendly enough, there seemed to be a conspiracy of silence where she's concerned. Which is a dichotomy, since you can't go in a gift shop anywhere in town without seeing Lady souvenirs."

"I suppose that's not surprising," she mused. "I've always found Ireland to be a land of contradictions. Since legends and tales have been retold and reshaped over so many years, it's only natural that they'd be more open to various viewpoints...

"There is something I've been wondering about since my walk," she said. "It dawned on me, when I came to the hedge blocking my way to the lake, that it wouldn't take that much for people to cut through it. Yet, looking at the castle and lake from the cottage window, or even a more expansive view from the hillside, there's no one there."

"That same thought occurred to me yesterday," Duncan said. "And I did find the reason for that. Whether locals believe it or simply use it to protect property, the story around the village is that the hedge is enchanted and that anyone who dares to cut through it will suffer a lifetime of terrible luck."

"They must tell it well," she decided.

"Enough that so far it seems to be working. Of course, all the farmers and garda who've been posted at various roadways to prevent trespassing this week undoubtedly help."

"After reading the book and seeing the movie, I'd like to believe in her," Cass admitted. "And if she does exist, it seems she deserves her privacy."

"You won't get any argument from me. So, does that mean that you're not going to write about her for your paper?"

"Probably not. I don't want to contribute to any more circus atmosphere like what I had to drive through as I was going through town."

"Still, it sounds as if this change in career has your writing in a good place... And speaking of your writing, you were talking about spinning off my bar misadventure into a story?"

"Not about you." She repeated what she'd told him earlier. "But about the serpent stowaway. I was thinking that when all the crews come ashore in New York, the serpent escapes the port to terrorize the city during Fleet Week."

"Along the lines of Jaws terrorizing Amity Island during the resort season."

"Exactly."

"Jaws was hard to find in the ocean. I can't see a sea serpent going unnoticed strolling down Broadway. I suppose it'd be too straightforward to just have a SWAT team shoot it?"

"Unfortunately, that wouldn't work. Because, having swum in the ocean where nuclear testing had taken place back in the 1950s, he's not only radioactive, but impervious to weapons of any kind."

"Like Spiderman. On steroids."

"Exactly," she repeated. As she turned toward him, her smile actually reached her eyes. "I considered having him fall in love with a Rockette while hiding out in Radio City Music Hall, and when the police try to capture it, it runs away, carrying his true love, and uses its tentacles to climb the lit-up Chrysler Building."

"That would certainly be dramatic."

"It's tempting. But I'm worried it's too over the top."

"You said you're supposed to stay away from anything resembling truth."

"True. And it's not like anything's over the top at the *Buzz*. So, while it's admittedly derivative of *King Kong*—"

"Which is why it would work," he decided as they passed a green fringe-topped pony cart carrying a family of sightseeing tourists. The driver of the cart, an elderly man wearing a tweed jacket over his sweater and wool pants and sporting a pair of tall kelly-green Wellies, waved as they went by.

"The premise was already set up for you by the movies," Duncan said. "And, since people have already shown themselves willing to buy that, they'll probably buy your serpent."

"I hope so. Dan definitely likes long-range prospects, so to drag the story out, as my flight passed over the North Pole, I envisioned the headlines, *FLEET WEEK CAPTIVE CARRYING ATOMIC SERPENT'S CHILD!!* But I'm worried that a woman having sex with a serpent is just too creepy."

Duncan rubbed his jaw. His stories had always been meant to leave people uncomfortable, to spotlight injustices around the world. As had hers. Now, it seemed her goal was to entertain and keep people reading. An idea he once would've scoffed at. But she wasn't the only one who'd changed. Although he hadn't been about to admit it to his godfather, it had occurred to him on more than one occasion the past months that he'd been skating that razor-thin line between dedication to his work and burnout.

"There is, admittedly, a cringe factor involved in that scenario," he allowed, putting his own issues aside for now. "But you already told readers your serpent has been affected by atomic waste. So, since everything on earth is made up of atoms, which make the molecules, which turn into cells, why can't you have the molecules and cells altered in a way that gave him the ability to shape-shift?"

"Oooh."

She twisted a curl in a familiar way as she considered that idea. He remembered when her hair had fallen past her shoulders and how, whenever she'd twist it while thinking, his gaze had automatically drifted down to her breasts.

Because, hey, even though he might have been approaching burnout, he was still a guy.

"I suppose I could have him morph into a vampire," she mused. "Though vamps have been done to death."

"No pun intended," Duncan said dryly, making her groan. "Maybe vampires have waned, but I'll bet no one's done a shape-shifting sea serpent vamp. After all, we've already established that you're writing to an audience who enjoys familiar stories."

"That's true. Then, give it five or six months, because, fortunately, *Buzz* readers seem incapable of keeping track of timelines—"

"And who the hell knows how long an atomic vampire sea serpent's gestation would be anyway?"

"Good point... So, after a few weeks or months, I could write the story of the baby's birth. But, oh, wait!" She clapped her hands, something she'd always done when she'd figured out the slant on a story. "Even better, before the birth, the paper could run a reader poll on whether the baby would be a girl or boy. Or more important, human or serpent/vamp shifter."

"Don't forget atomic or non-atomic."

"Absolutely." Duncan could see the wheels turning in her head. "In fact, what if, like The Hulk, he doesn't really have control of the change? What if he could be a vampire one day, then change into a huge, scaly serpent with a temper the next?"

"The possibilities are endless."

"Thank you." The throaty warmth in her voice had him considering pulling the car over. Now. "Being able to discuss it with another writer helped me with just the details I need to weave it all together."

"My pleasure." He reached out his left hand and linked their fingers together over the console as they drove across the stone bridge into town. "We always made a good team. I'd get bogged down in minutia, while you'd always find a way to give a piece a more personal, emotional touch."

"We did work well together." Her eyes turned reminiscent, which, along with her not pulling her hand away, gave him the impression that she was finally remembering some good times between them. "On the rare occasion we were in the same place at the same time."

"I've wondered about that," Duncan admitted. "If things would've turned out differently if you'd have come to work with me at GNN."

And you wouldn't have been in Egypt. At least without me to keep you safe, like I did the day we met, he thought but did not say. Duncan had considered that possibility countless times over the past months, and even knowing that just wanting to protect his wife hadn't been any guarantee that he actually *could* have, he continued to blame himself for not having been there when she needed him.

"We both know I only received that offer from Winston because I was married to you."

Like all journalists, she had her pride. But in this case, she was wrong. "Believe me, I had nothing to do with it. He wanted to hire you because not only does a good-looking woman in a war zone win ratings points, you were a great writer.

"And still are," he tacked on, not wanting her to think he was putting down her current work. Especially now that he knew why she'd accepted the job at the tabloid and realized how much time and creative thought went into crafting her outlandish stories. Which wasn't surprising, since, until Egypt, she'd never done anything halfway.

"It wouldn't have worked," she said softly, demonstrating that he hadn't been the only one to wonder.

He shrugged and felt a pang of loss as she retrieved her hand. "Well, we'll never know, will we?

"So," he said, wanting to move the topic away from their foreign work, which inevitably led back to that debacle in Egypt, "getting back to your writing, have you considered picking your novel up again?"

"I think about it from time to time," she said as they reached the village.

In normal times, the tidy fifteenth-century town with its bright storefronts, artistically hand-painted signs, and stone church could have looked like a poster from the Irish Tourism Bureau. The crowds filling the cobblestone sidewalks and spilling into the street took away from the ambiance, giving it more of a carnival flavor.

"But it was autobiographical, as most first novels probably are," she continued as he braked for a portly man laden down with a plethora of professional camera equipment. "And it would probably have a better chance of selling if I kept it that way. But my heart isn't into writing or even thinking about my journalism days."

"That's understandable." He was also starting to think that this might be another thing they had in common. "Ireland's known for its writers and poets. Maybe there's something in the air that will help you find a new direction."

"That's a thought," she allowed. Then, as he glanced over at her again, without warning, humor sparkled in her eyes. "Maybe I'll write about a leprechaun vampire."

They shared a laugh as he pulled into a parking space across from the pub and cut the engine. He turned toward her, and as their eyes met, for this one suspended moment, the past dark months spun away, and instead of sitting in a rental car while the Irish rain fell and the fog blew in from the sea, they were standing on a sundrenched beach, so in love Duncan had wondered if a heart could actually burst from an excess of joy.

It was a feeling he'd never known until he'd met Cass.

Their eyes met. And held.

Duncan dipped his head.

Cass's lips parted.

Heaven was a mere breath away when she drew back and reached for the door handle. "We'd better get going before someone claims our table."

He could change her mind. Duncan knew that it would only take a touch here...a stroke of his fingertips there...a long, slow, wet kiss, and she'd be willing to go with him into the mists.

But he'd come to realize, during his conversations with her cousin, that from the moment they'd met, he'd been the one convincing her to go along with his plans. Now, rather than settle for immediate gratification, he was going to have to play the long game and wait for her to be the one to make the move.

Hopefully sooner rather than later. Before his balls turned as blue as a Smurf.

13

CASSANDRA FELT AS if she'd stumbled into a scene from *The Quiet Man*. Or at the very least, the way the pub was filled to the high-beamed rafters with memorabilia, some of which looked as if it had been new in earlier centuries, an Irish folk museum. One vintage sign announced a *Post Office and Radio Service*, another recommended *Guinness for Strength*, and yet another—an obviously newer-era chalkboard hung up beside the coat rack on the wall—read in bold white script, *No Wifi. Talk to each other!*

"I like that one," she said as Duncan helped her out of her coat and hung it up on one of the wooden pegs.

"The other times I've been here, it listed the daily specials," he told her.

"That would be Elizabeth Murphy," a dark-haired man said as he walked past with a tray of pints. He pointed toward a small, birdlike woman who looked as if Willard Scott should be sending her a centenarian birthday card. "She's been Castlelough postmistress for more years than anyone can remember. She also has a powerful dislike of people reading and texting on their smartphones during a *seisiún*."

"Good for her," Cass said, smiling at the woman whose raven bright eyes suddenly turned toward her as she tuned up a fiddle that appeared to be even older than she was.

Elizabeth Murphy did not smile back. But she did put down her bow to wave Cass and Duncan over.

"You'd best do as instructed," the man with the pints suggested. "If you'd want to be receiving mail any time in this century."

"Do people actually still send mail?" Cassandra asked.

His smile was quick and warm. "Not as much as they once did. Which may make her work easier, but the cutback on people visiting her office has affected her gossip, which, in turn, has proven a problem because she's always considered serving as village crier to be part and parcel of her postmistress. Meanwhile, her nemesis, Mrs. Sheehan, who runs the butcher shop and is another who never would keep news, or her thoughts, for that matter, to herself, has been giving her a run for her money."

"If what the *Castlelough Celtic* published in this week's edition is any indication, they don't have a great deal of competition," Duncan said.

"Aye. That's true enough." The man nodded. "Dermott Moroney was once a fine newsman. But he's not as young as he once was, and with his heart set on trading in our Irish sunshine for the warmer and drier Greek version, it's obvious to one and all that he's lost interest in the paper.

"I'm Patrick Brennan, proprietor and brewmaster," he belatedly introduced himself to Cassandra. "And you'd be this boyo's wife everyone has been waiting to meet."

"Cassandra Carpenter." She managed an answering

smile even as her fears about Duncan having made them the center of attention seemed to be proving true. "And yes, this boyo"—despite her discomfort, she couldn't help shooting Duncan a teasing glance—"is my husband."

"It's grand to meet you, Cassandra Carpenter," Patrick Brennan said.

"Patrick," the older woman called out. "Why don't you deliver those pints and quit bending the girl's ear, so I can be meeting her."

"Aye, Mrs. Murphy," Patrick called back. "Don't forget," he told Duncan, "the snug's in the back when you want a bit of privacy and quiet."

As if sensing her nerves, Duncan took her hand as they wove through the crowd that had come to hear the music. Given the number of tourists she'd seen earlier, Cass was surprised that, except for Duncan and her, they all appeared to be locals.

Elizabeth Murphy was wearing a white blouse with a lacy tie, a green tartan skirt that fell to her ankles, and the type of black lace-up shoes a nun might have worn. She gave Cassandra a long look from the top of her head down to the pointed toes of her red boots, then back up again.

"You'd be the bride this one made the romantic breakfast for," she said.

Deciding not to get into an argument about whether or not she'd considered the breakfast romantic, which, dammit, she actually had, Cassandra merely said, "Last I heard, I was the only wife he has."

The stern look dissolved as the woman cackled. "And why would he make any other when he has such a lovely wife? I like your hair. I, personally, am too old to change my ways, so I'll be sticking with my bun." She patted the steely bun in question. "But if I were younger, I might let Moira Kelly, the lass who runs Hair Holiday by the harbor, take her scissors to me."

"I think you look very elegant just the way you are," Duncan said.

"Oh, my. Aren't you the charmer? Just like my late husband, Doyle," she said on what came close to a girlish giggle. "You'd best keep him," she advised Cassandra. "While charmingly cocky men can be a challenge, you'll never lack for compliments. Not that you don't deserve them... The pair of you will make beautiful children."

The breath backed up in Cassandra's lungs at that, but as Duncan reassuringly squeezed her fingers, she reminded herself to breathe. Surprisingly, unlike when she couldn't bear to have him in the same apartment, for some reason she'd think about later tonight, when she was alone and her thoughts weren't spinning, right now she found his presence eased the loss she'd come to accept would always be a part of her.

"Thank you," she said mildly.

"Well, it's been lovely to meet you, Mrs. Murphy," Duncan said as the woman tilted her head and, as if sensing something amiss, gave Cassandra a sharper, more probing look. "But we'd best let you warm up for the session. Hopefully we'll be seeing you again."

"Oh, you can count on that," Elizabeth Murphy said. "I hope you'll enjoy the *craic*," she tacked on as she went back to tuning the fiddle.

Just as Patrick Brennan had promised, the snug door had a *reserved* sign on it. It wasn't large—just a booth and a pair of wooden benches that looked as if they might have been reclaimed from one of the many stone churches Cassandra had passed on her drive to Castlelough—but set in the back of the pub as it was, it offered privacy while allowing them to see the wooden dance floor where the musicians were setting up.

"I'm sorry about that," he said as they sat across from each other.

Cassandra shrugged. "She had no way of knowing. She was being kind."

"But it still hurts."

"Yes," she said softly. "It does."

"And I suspect it always will," Duncan said. In the beginning, he'd told himself that he'd suffered in silence in order to not make Cass's pain even worse. Then, as the days went on, he'd used the excuse of her having retreated even deeper into that remote, icy shell. How could they have a conversation, he'd reasoned, if she refused to say a damn word?

But he'd belatedly accepted that the reason he'd remained silent was that it hurt too much. And even if she *had* been willing to talk about the miscarriage, he'd have had not a clue what to say. Especially since the one thing his numbnuts brain had come up, the promise of another child, had only made things even worse.

He'd told himself when he heard she was coming that he was going to take things slow. Not force her into a discussion that she wasn't ready for. But he could see for himself that Sedona Sullivan had been right about her having gotten stronger.

Having vowed, during the long, sleepless night waiting for her arrival, that he was going to be totally honest this time and not hold anything back, he decided the time had come to share something personal that he'd never told anyone.

"My mother had a miscarriage."

She'd obviously been stumbling into telling Cass herself, that night she'd called while sounding as if were making her way through a bottle of Bombay Sapphire. He'd known that her call had been well intended, but her timing and delivery had sucked. Which was why he'd abruptly cut her off before she'd gotten to the crying jag. Which Cassandra so hadn't needed.

She turned toward him, her surprise obvious.

"She did? When?"

"The summer I turned thirteen." And all these years later, talking about those days still tangled his gut into knots.

His mother had called her pregnancy a surprise miracle, seemingly excited at the prospect of dirty diapers, a crying infant, and no sleep. Of course, the McCaraghs could easily afford to hire a nanny to take over the unpleasant parts of parenting. But one night, Duncan had been awakened by a loud argument about his mother's desire to tend to her child herself. It had been the first time he'd ever heard his coolly remote father raise his voice.

The following morning at breakfast, his mother's eyes had been red-rimmed, but she'd kept the appointment with the first of the selection of nanny prospects the gold-star employment agency had lined up.

"That's quite a gap between children," Cass said.

"It was. And being a teenager, not to mention an only child, I'll admit that I wasn't looking forward to the changes an infant would bring to our lives."

"Your life," she guessed.

"Bulls-eye. You never knew my mother before."

"I don't know her now," Cass pointed out.

"Touché." It was something he was going to have to figure out. Later. "She was a warm, outgoing woman who filled our home with sunshine."

"Really."

It was not a question, but he heard the skepticism in her tone. "Really. It was only after I'd grown up that I realized how much of an effort she'd made to try to compensate for my father's coldness.

"Anyway, I'll admit to being mad as hell. But there must have been a lot of chapters on sibling rivalry in all those baby books she bought, because she spent her pregnancy lavishing me with extra attention."

"That's sweet," Cass said, even as her eyes shone with moisture. Worrying that his timing sucked as badly as his mother's drunken phone call, Duncan experienced a wave of relief as Patrick Brennan knocked on the door before opening it to ask if they'd like something from the bar.

After a bit of discussion, they ordered a pint of the Brennan Brewery Brian Boru Black Ale for Duncan, Pirate Queen Red Ale for Cass, a deep-fried St. Brigid's cheese appetizer, and cod and chips with lemon aioli to share.

"I hope all that fried food comes with a defibrillator for the heart attack we're risking," Cass murmured after Patrick left with their order.

"Don't worry. If you do happen to be struck down with a heart attack, I know CPR."

"I'll bet you do." The tears that had been threatening turned to indulgent laughter. "Mrs. Murphy was right. You're a cocky charmer *and* a challenge. You just want to get your hands on my chest."

"Guilty as charged." He flashed a grin. "And feel free to do the same to me if I keel over."

She tilted her head. Chewed thoughtfully on an unpainted nail. "I'll consider it."

Duncan was remembering all too well how those slender, long-fingered hands had felt on his chest. His abs. And lower still.

Damn. He wasn't sure about charming. But as the five metal buttons pulled at the denim of his jeans, he'd definitely turned achingly cocky.

And from the teasing smile in her eyes and the hint of a dimple he hadn't seen since their honeymoon, she knew exactly how that finger in her mouth thing had affected him.

"Now who's making the move?" he asked.

"Tit for tat," she responded. Then blushed as she realized the unplanned double entendre.

Despite what had begun as a serious topic, Duncan couldn't hold back his grin. "That's too easy, even for a cocky charmer like me."

They were seated across an old wooden farm table from each other, the vibes bouncing back and forth the same way they had over dinner that first night in Kabul. But along with the heat, there was something else going on here. Friendship. And once again, the deep emotional connection that he'd been missing for so long.

"This is nice," she said. "I'm glad you talked me into it."

"Me, too." Unable to resist, he reached across the table, cupped her cheek in his hand, and felt it warm his palm.

"Duncan."

"It's not a move." She felt so soft. So familiar. The ache returned. In his heart and in his groin.

"I wasn't complaining. I was just telling you that our beer's here."

He turned and followed her gaze to the door, where Patrick Brennan stood with the green metal tray holding their ales, appetizer, and two side plates. Once again he seemed undecided whether or not to interrupt.

Duncan waved him in.

"Sorry," he said.

"No problem," Duncan assured him. If nothing else, the beer would hopefully lower his body heat to something a few degrees cooler than the Sahara in summer. "That looks great."

"The cheese is from Michael's farm. There are some who say that his Camembert is the best in all Ireland."

"I have a question," Cass asked as he placed the glasses and plates on the table. "It's obvious your pub is successful."

"It does well enough," Patrick said mildly.

"So many locals being here tonight attest to that. So," she asked, "where are all the tourists?"

"I wouldn't know, but my guess is that they're at The Irish Rose, given that it's declared itself *Lady Central* with all sorts of raffles, giveaways, theme nights and other such inducements, which isn't my business style.

"The Irish Rose was the only other pub in the village while I was growing up. Then Brendan O'Neill, who'd taken over from his father, moved to America. An O'Neill cousin tried to make a go of it, but unfortunately he enjoyed his Guinness a bit too much, so the business was failing. I'd already established my microbrewery and was in the process of buying him out so I'd have a place to serve my own beers, when a wealthy American came to town with a hefty checkbook and all sorts of grandiose plans to turn The Rose into an American style Irish pub."

"Isn't that a contradiction?" Duncan suggested. "Like the old 'carrying coals to Newcastle' expression?"

"Aye. You'd think so, wouldn't you? But Desmond— he'd be the cousin—didn't care about that as much as he did scoring himself a grand payday. So, despite us having a verbal agreement, he sold to the American.

"Which turned out for the best, given that this larger building came available the very next week. It had gone vacant and fallen into disrepair after the collapse of the Celtic Tiger, so I managed to negotiate a good price and had Bram, my builder brother, bring it back to what it once was."

"Bram was the one who restored Briarwood Cottage," Duncan told Cass.

"Really?" Her eyes lit up. "He did a wonderful job! The moment I walked in this morning, I felt as if I'd come home."

"And isn't that the point of any house?" Patrick asked. "To make it feel like home? At any rate, after I opened for business, the locals migrated here, while The Irish Rose has, in turn, carved out a fine tourism business for itself."

"Sounds like a win/win for you both," Cass said.

"It is, indeed," Patrick agreed with a bold smile that revealed his pride in Brennan's. "And now I'd best be about getting your dinner made. Enjoy your ale and cheese."

Once they were alone again, a companionable quiet

settled over Duncan and Cass as she split the appetizer onto the two smaller plates.

"To being back in the Emerald Island," Duncan risked saying as he lifted his glass of dark ale. "Together again."

She hesitated a heartbeat. Then lifted her own glass. "To being back here."

Duncan duly noted that she hadn't added the part about being back together, but since she'd already said she was glad he'd talked her into coming here tonight, he was feeling a great deal more positive than he had even twenty-four hours ago.

"You were telling me about your mother," she reminded him, proving that her depression hadn't had any long-term effect on that steel-trap mind he'd always admired.

"Yeah." Buying time to drag his mind back to that topic that, on his list of least favorite things, would rank between waterboarding and spending eternity locked in a room watching Justin Bieber music videos, Duncan took a long drink of ale.

"Like I said, I was jealous. So, in retaliation, I became more and more like my father."

She eyed him over the rim of her glass. "How? I don't know your father, either," she reminded him.

Cass might currently be writing tabloid *gee whiz* stories, but she still thought like a journalist. Every statement risked a follow-up question. "I started distancing myself from her. Became cooler and monosyllabic. Which, looking back, was cruel."

"You were thirteen," she reminded him. "Not exactly the age of reason. It could have been more because of your age. I remember boys I'd grown up with becoming nearly mute once hormones started kicking in."

"It's a nice excuse. But the fact was, I was pretty much just a douche."

Duncan still remembered the way his mother had laughed with almost giddy pleasure between contractions as she left their Main Line home for the hospital. He hadn't exactly resisted when she'd hugged him good-bye. But he had stiffened and held his arms at his sides.

Even worse than the remembered resentment was the guilt he'd suffered when she'd returned home the next day, pale and wan, without her surprise miracle baby.

Having experienced the loss of a child from the father's perspective, Duncan now wondered if perhaps his father's pain had been the reason he'd grown increasing colder. Why he'd distanced himself even further from his wife and son.

Whatever the reason, his mother had been left to deal with her loss on her own. Which was when she'd found comfort in alcohol.

"That was what she was going to tell me, wasn't it?" Cassandra asked quietly, showing that her reporter skills of listening to what *wasn't* said were still as strong as ever.

"Yeah. Probably." He sighed heavily even as he could hear the joyful sounds of a reel being played out in the main part of the pub. "Since I could tell she'd been drinking and I wasn't sure how the call was going to turn out, I decided it wasn't the way you needed to hear the story."

"She wanted to let me know I wasn't alone." Duncan could tell that Cass was surprised by that.

"Yeah."

"So, she turned to alcohol to ease the pain. And got

stuck in her own sad limbo."

"That's one way of putting it. And I blame myself for not knowing how to fix her."

"You were young," she repeated. "Besides, I've already learned that no one can fix anyone. We all have to fix ourselves." She ran a fingernail around the rim of the glass Patrick had poured her ale into. "But I was more fortunate than most. Because I had you. And Sedona."

"Yeah, I proved a helluva lot of help," he ground out, deciding that banging his head onto the scarred wooden table wouldn't exactly add anything to this long-overdue discussion. I want you to know that, as soon as the words about having another child came out of my mouth, I realized that I'd sounded unbelievably insensitive. At the time I was so totally numb—"

"You were?" He could tell that was the biggest surprise of the night.

"As a stone."

"But you took care of making the travel arrangements out of Egypt, you booked the flights, you made the doctor appointments, you cooked. You did *everything.*"

"If there's one thing going days or weeks without sleep has taught me, it's how to operate on autopilot." He dragged his hands down his face. Sighed heavily. "Which I was pretty much doing back then. But I did know I'd screwed up when I heard those words, which were meant to encourage both of us, coming out of my damn idiot mouth."

Cassandra belatedly realized that he'd been trying to convince not just her but *himself* that life could go on. That someday they'd be, maybe not entirely normal, but their version of it, again.

She'd watched Ducan with refugees fleeing both war zones and natural disasters, wounded children in makeshift shelters, women who'd been held captive by terrorists, and so many other unspeakable human casualties born of a dangerous world. Even as he'd never fail to get the story he'd come to tell, he'd also be so gentle. So caring.

As he'd been with her.

If she'd only been thinking clearly, Cass would have realized what he'd been trying to say. Instead, even as she'd begun to recover, as recently as two days ago, that one ill-timed comment had continued to ache like a sore tooth.

This time it was Cassandra who reached out to take *his* hand. "You were trying to give us both hope."

As was his nature. She'd often wondered how such a warm man had come from that seemingly icy family. Having heard the damage Angela McCaragh's miscarriage had caused to his family, she now decided that he'd either inherited or learned his kindness and sensitivity from his mother.

"I was searching for some glimmer of hope," he admitted as his thumb traced little circles on the sensitive skin of her palm. "Which turned out to be a major fail."

"It wasn't your fault."

"Nor yours."

And wasn't that what Sedona and Dr. Fletcher had been telling her? And although Cassandra had wanted to believe them, a very strong part of her had been clinging to that dark guilt she'd wrapped around herself like a shroud.

"Okay." She exhaled a long breath. "We've talked

enough about sad things for one night," she decided. "We're here in the most beautiful spot on earth, there's great food, music playing, and people dancing, so why don't we put those days aside for now and enjoy our evening?"

He lifted her hand to his lips. "Deal."

14

I F IT WAS true that the traditional music of a country reflected the songs the people all carried in their hearts, Cassandra decided that the music being played in Brennan's reflected the Irish landscape. As the informal gathering of fiddlers, flutists, drummers, whistlers, and guitar and concertina players entertained, she could picture dizzyingly tall cliffs looking out over the Atlantic toward America; wild winter surf; rolling green fields separated by stone fences where sheep and cattle grazed; the busy harbor where fishermen arrived from the sea to deliver their catch to the restaurants and fish mongers; the reed-fringed Lough Caislean with its castle ruins, along with whitewashed cottages and brightly painted buildings that offered such a cheery contrast to the gray of the sea and sky. It was all there, in the music and lyrics—the kings and castles, battles and banishments, the magic and miracles.

They'd finished their dinner, and lured by the evocative music, she was sitting on a stool against a far wall, Duncan beside her, when a man who appeared to be even older than Elizabeth Murphy came dancing over to her, took hold of her hand, and, although he appeared to be nearly a foot shorter than her own five foot four and may have possibly weighed a hundred pounds soaking wet, he nevertheless proved strong enough to pull her off the wooden stool.

"Come dance with me, darlin'," he said.

"I don't know the steps." As opposed to the others, who looked as if they'd been performing those steps since childhood.

"Ah, now, it's not about the order you get the steps in," he assured her. "All you do is do what your heart tells you, and we'll be turning you into a pro jigger in no time at all."

As he proceeded to drag her across the floor, she glanced back at Duncan, who was off his own stool and headed her way. When she shook her head to let him know his protection wasn't necessary, he lifted a dark brow, then shrugged and stood there, arms crossed, watching as she and her partner twirled and skipped around like mad fools while the others laughed and applauded their encouragement.

"My name is Fergus," he told her as he spun her out, then pulled her back again without missing a beat. "And you'd be Cassandra. Wife of the famous television journalist, Duncan McCaragh."

"Duncan is my husband," she confirmed as he spun her in a tight series of dizzying circles.

"He seems like a fine man. For a Scotsman."

"A Scotsman who'd like to dance with his wife," Duncan's deep voice said behind her.

"And aren't you a fortunate fellow," Fergus said, handing her over as if she had no say in the matter.

"And don't I know it," Duncan agreed. As he took Cassandra into his arms, the music changed from an energetic reel to a lyrical air that reminded her of the walk she'd taken earlier, where the cemetery and the cairn had invited her to slow down and breathe.

"You both behaved as if I were a horse being sold at Sunday market," she complained without heat.

"And should I not have agreed that I'm fortunate to have such a winsome wife?" he asked on an exaggerated brogue that had her fighting back a laugh. "And believe me, darling, I'm well aware that you're no horse but a very hot female."

She shook her head as she twined her arms around his neck. "If I were keeping score, I'd feel the need to point out that's getting close to a move."

"No." As he turned her in a slow circle, he pulled her closer against his still very fine, hard body. "Now this," he murmured as he bent his head and nibbled on her earlobe, which only he had ever discovered possessed a direct connection to her nipples, "is a move."

He'd always been an excellent dancer, in part because of the lessons he'd told her he'd been forced to take as part of his boyhood etiquette instruction. He turned her beneath his raised arm with an easy male grace, then pulled her back in, fitting her even tighter against him than before.

His smooth-moving feet weren't the only thing in motion, she realized as those metal buttons pressed against her, causing too-long neglected parts of her body to do a happy dance of their own.

They'd danced for their first and, until tonight, last time together on the beach after their wedding. The resort staff had returned to work, the minister had left for wherever the concierge had found her, and the vacationers who'd been baking their bodies in the sun while drinking mai tais all day must have gone inside to party in one of the many bars.

They'd been all alone, swaying together barefoot in the sand, Duncan humming Adele's "Make You Feel My Love" while a huge white moon floated overhead. At the time, when he'd requested the song, Cassandra had considered it an easy choice given that it had been one of the most popular wedding songs of the year.

But now, looking back on it, he'd been echoing the vows he'd written on the flight to the island. The ones he'd reminded her of earlier today. Had it only been one day? Like the lyrics said, the winds of change were definitely blowing wild and free.

She leaned her head back to look up at him. "You chose that song on purpose, didn't you?"

He didn't pretend to believe that she might be talking about how the musicians had segued from "The South Wind" to the even more haunting "She Moved Through the Fair."

"I did. Because I meant those words then and I meant them this morning. There is *nothing* I wouldn't do to make you feel my love."

The fierce heat in his eyes and rumbled baritone that strummed at least a gazillion strings had Cassandra almost dissolving into a puddle of need right on the dance floor. How was it that just days ago, she'd considered going to dinner with Sedona and her friends a major achievement? But now, here on this very public dance floor, she was on the verge of tearing off her husband's clothes and climbing up his body right here in Brennan's in front of nearly the entire population of Castlelough.

Before Egypt she'd never been able to resist this man.

After Egypt just the sight of Duncan struggling to make things right had caused her heart to ache even worse than when she'd learned about their baby.

Now, even as she tried to tell herself that it was only sexual chemistry intensified by months of celibacy, Cassandra knew what was happening between them was much, much more.

"Ah," she tried for humor as she barely resisted biting that square jaw that had been chiseled by more than his fair share of testosterone, "is *that* what I'm feeling?"

"Like most guys, the good Lord only gave me enough blood for my head or my penis," he growled into her ear, not that anyone could hear them now that the musicians had moved on to a lively jig even as she and Duncan continued to sway in place, surrounded by energetic Riverdance wannabes. "Which means that any doctor in the country would probably declare me brain-dead right now."

He'd always been able to make her laugh.

Until he hadn't.

But then, miracle of miracles, he did again.

"Well then," she said, giving into impulse and going up on her toes to nip that sexily stubbled jaw, "I suppose we'd best get you home."

He went as still as one of those ancient Celtic stones surrounding the cairn as he gave her a long, speculative look. "Are you saying—"

"Brain death is not to be taken lightly." It had been so long since she'd flirted. Too long. Cassandra had forgotten the fun in tongue-tying a strong, confident alpha male. "We could call the local doctor. Or…"

She skimmed her index finger down the front of his shirt, pausing to toy with his belt buckle. "We could go back to the cottage, put you to bed, and try some old-fashioned home remedies."

He covered her hand with his. "I vote for number two."

She felt those unused muscles beside her mouth stretch as she smiled again. "Good choice."

Arms wrapped around each other, they stumbled across the street to the parking space like two drunks holding each other up. Which, except for the drunk part, was mostly true.

The rental beeped as he unlocked it with the remote, then, with a broad palm cupping her butt, he boosted her into the high passenger seat. Her girly parts had given up their happy dance and were now shouting at her to satisfy them. Had it not been for the streetlight shining into the SUV, she might have actually seriously considered doing exactly that here and now.

After settling into the driver's seat and starting the engine, before shifting into reverse, he turned toward her. "I don't suppose you happen to have brought along one of those tight nurse outfits with the lace garter belts, white, lace-topped stockings, and do-me-big-boy stilettos?"

"Sorry. Frederick's of Hollywood hasn't reached Shelter Bay yet."

He shrugged. "No problem. You've always been hot to me whatever you're wearing." He waggled wicked brows. "Or not wearing."

"This is crazy," she said breathlessly.

"Insane," he agreed. "The plan was to get our marriage situation worked out before we moved on to screwing each other's brains out."

And didn't that suggestion cause vital body parts to spike? But...

"You actually had this all planned out?"

"I'm a Marine," he reminded her. "We always have a plan."

Which put him miles ahead of her. Cassandra hadn't even come up with what to say when he'd opened the door.

She could have felt manipulated. But instead, as they drove away from the lights of the village, headed back toward Briarwood Cottage, she said, "Sometimes, going off plan can turn out to be a good thing."

"Oorah," Duncan agreed.

15

A S THEY PULLED up in front of the cottage, the lights in the window gleaming a warm welcome, Duncan turned toward Cassandra.

"Are you sure about this?"

There might be many things she didn't have a handle on, but about this, Cassandra was absolutely, one-hundred-and-a-gazillion percent positive. "Absolutely."

His face, shadowed as clouds drifted across the moon, revealed a hesitation she hadn't expected. The one thing that had always been good between them was the sex. Not that they'd had any since the last time they'd been in Ireland.

"No regrets," he warned.

She shook her head and kissed him. A long, deep, breath-stealing kiss. "No regrets," she echoed when they finally came up for air. "I want you to take me to bed, Duncan." She pressed a hand against his chest and felt his heart beating as hard and fast as one of the bodhran drums at the session. Once again in sync, its rhythm echoed that of her own wild, reckless heart. "Now."

They were no steadier making their way from the SUV to the cottage than they'd been leaving the pub. As soon as they got inside, he spun her around, pressed her against the blue door, and dove back into the interrupted kiss.

Cass followed him willingly as tongues tangled, teeth scraped, heat flared. When his fingers took hold of her short curls and pulled her head back, allowing access to her throat, her entire world narrowed down to his mouth and hands, which were cupping her breasts while his thumbs rubbed her nipples. Which were, unfortunately, covered by that sweater dress she'd thought was so pretty when Sedona had talked her into buying it.

"You're wearing too many clothes." He read her reeling thoughts.

He lowered those wonderfully wicked hands to the hem of her dress and lifted it up her legs. "Raise your arms."

She raised them above her head, wiggling her hips a bit as he peeled it up over her head and threw it across the room.

Then, before she could rip away his shirt so she could feel them skin to skin, his mouth took hers again, his hands streaking over her, causing flames to shoot through her veins as he nudged her legs apart, then moved between them, his hard, urgent erection pressing against her, causing her lower body to throb.

"Damn, I've missed this." His breath was harsh. Ragged. "Missed the way you feel," he said as he undid her bra and claimed her breasts with first his hands and then his hot and hungry mouth.

Her underpants went next. Then, needing to touch him as he was touching her, she slid her hands up beneath his shirt to touch hot flesh.

It was crazy. Insane. Incredible.

She hadn't even realized what a dry, empty spell she'd been in until all it took was his hand cupping her, and the stroke of a clever thumb at the same time his teeth tugged on an ultrasensitive nipple to send her over the edge.

She was not alone in her hunger. Her gasp, then shuddering moan fueled his own demand as he kissed her again, his mouth hard. Hungry.

"I wanted to do this right," Duncan ground out as he yanked open the buttons on his 501s. "Take things slow. Seduce you."

"I don't need seduction." What she needed was that bold, hard nine inches she now wondered how and *why* she'd gone so long without. He jerked in her hand as she wrapped her fingers around him, stroking him in a familiar way that had him yanking a condom from his pocket and tearing the package open with his teeth. The first time she'd witnessed that raw male hunger was the night they'd met in Kabul. Knowing that she was the one who could drive him to such extremes only made her own fires flare hotter.

Cupping her butt, he lifted her off her feet and entered her with one stroke that had her crying out his name. Then he began to move, and as she wrapped her legs around his hips and was dragged into that spinning, whirling place where only he'd ever been able to take her, Cassandra's last coherent thought was that the cottage could burn down around them, and neither of them would ever notice.

It didn't take long. Only a few hard, deep strokes for him to find his own release, at the same time she felt herself breaking apart.

Somehow, when she'd floated back to earth, they were

lying on the wooden floor. As her head cleared, she realized that she was completely naked. Well, almost.

"I'm still wearing my boots."

He pressed his lips against her throat and caused her cooling blood to heat again. Then glanced down at her, giving her a lazy, lustful study that had her toes curling in those red boots. "It's a good look," he decided. "I think you ought to keep it."

"And wouldn't that cause a stir down at Brennan's?"

His hand settled between her legs with an easy familiarity that was at odds with the fact that it had been months since they'd been this way together. "I had in mind something a little more personal. That you stay that way for me."

"All the time?"

He glanced over at her. "You have a problem with that idea?"

"Actually, I do. Are you trying to tell me something?"

"Yeah. I like sex. With my wife. Who I've really missed seeing naked, so I figure we've got some time to make up for."

"So you haven't turned into one of those guys with a dungeon?"

"What the hell are you talking about?"

"I take it that's a no," she decided as he jerked his hand away from where, if she were to be perfectly honest, it had felt good. Really, really good.

"Where did that idea come from?"

"Well, you know. I've been reading how BDSM seems to have become a popular way to jazz up sex these days, so I just thought, just perhaps, you'd taken it up." His answering glower could have cut through steel. "I guess not," she said.

"Definitely not." He began making little circles on the damp inside of her thigh. "And we never had to play any games to jazz up our sex. But if the idea turns you on, hey, I'd be willing to give it the old college try."

"That's okay." She wiggled a bit to encourage him to move those fingers up and over just a bit. "I'm pretty much a vanilla girl."

His earlier annoyance dissolved as he flashed her a wicked grin. "That's always been my favorite flavor." To prove the point, he shifted positions and planted his mouth where his hand had been.

Which essentially put an end to the conversation.

16

THEY'D FINALLY MADE it to the bed, where they spent the night making up for lost time. The sun had begun to rise in the sky outside the window when Cassandra opened her eyes. "I dreamed of something last night."

Duncan put his arm around her and tugged her close. Although he'd lost track of the number of times she'd come, and his own count had been a personal best, he was already wanting her again. "In the all of ten minutes you slept?"

"Hah hah." She playfully slapped his upper arm in a way that reminded him of his old Cass. "What makes you think I didn't doze off during one of those times when you thought I was just dazed with lust?"

"Maybe because everyone down at Brennan's probably heard you screaming my name? Along with 'Take me now, you damn barbarian Scotsman'?"

"I said that?"

"Actually, you shouted it. And while I like to believe I have a fairly strong ego, it would sting a bit to discover that you've been using my body to have sex with Gerard Butler."

"Of course I didn't do that. Though, and I really don't

want to hurt your feelings, because you're a fabulous lover, there are admittedly times, occasionally, when I fantasize about you wearing a kilt."

Duncan felt his face splitting into a bold Highlander's grin. "I'll go out and get one today."

"You wouldn't get any objection from me. And I couldn't have been *that* loud."

"Sweetheart, they're going to be finding bits of thatch all over Castlelough." He glanced up at the ceiling. "Because I think we may have blown the roof off."

"Well, then, you'll just have to go up there and fix it. While wearing your new McCaragh kilt. While I stand down on the ground and watch." She laughed and snuggled closer, her hand on his chest. "You know how often dreams don't make any sense when you've been awake awhile?"

"Sure." The past few years *his* dreams had been more the stuff of nightmares. Of a continually changing kaleidoscope of images that hadn't made any sense when he'd witnessed them in real life.

"Well, this one keeps calling to me."

"That's always a plus." Duncan was not going to think about those bad times. Instead he was going to focus on being back in bed with his wife.

"It is. I was thinking that perhaps, rather than write a novel about a female journalist, which had been my original idea—"

"Going along with the old 'write what you know' adage." He touched his lips to the top of her head, breathing in the crisp citrus scent of her shampoo.

"That's what they say. Whoever *they* are. But I've no desire to relive my journalism days, so I was thinking more along the lines of a fictionalized version of what's happening here. Of some sort of event that could be considered by many to be miraculous. And how that changes the people who live in the small, isolated town where the miracle occurs while also changing those who witnessed it."

"That's not a bad idea." Although fiction might not be his strong suit, Duncan could see Cass making it work.

"As I said, I'm still just playing with what-ifs."

"You'd probably want to stay here a while," he suggested carefully. Like a month, for starters. "Getting a better handle on the town and residents would give your story more verisimilitude, making it more realistic and believable even though it'd clearly be fiction."

"I loved how Quinn Gallagher had me suspending disbelief when he wrote about the Lady," Cass said. "Since I felt I knew the people and the setting, I was able to accept the idea of an underground kingdom beneath the lake and scientists trying to capture her… Maybe once the Lady seekers leave town, I can find a flat to rent," she mused.

Or move in with me.

"Sounds as if you've pretty much made up your mind."

"Not quite yet. But I'm getting closer."

"Maybe some local color will help," Duncan said.

"That's a good idea," she agreed.

"So, I have a proposition for you."

"Anything," she said.

"Great. We can stop for breakfast on the way."

"On the way? Where are we going?"

"To the Lahinch Surf Shop."

Her gaze cut to the window, where the day had dawned bright and so atypically sunny Duncan could picture people stumbling around the streets of Castlelough, hands over their eyes, looking up toward the robin's-egg-blue sky while crying out, "I've gone blind! Blind, I tell you!"

"You're proposing we go surfing?" she asked.

"Yeah. We had fun the last time, so I thought it might be worth trying again. I went online to check while you were knocked out, and although surfing here on the west coast can be iffier than the east where we were before, thanks to the wind changing, the waves are going to be clean and glassy until late afternoon."

"Which is a good thing?"

"A very good thing. They'll be perfect for a novice, but you don't have to worry, because I won't let you fall."

"I thought you were supposed to be writing a story for Winston."

"I only need one a week." He snapped his fingers. "Piece of cake." Leaning down, Duncan nuzzled her neck. "Come on, my little beach bunny," he coaxed. "Play hooky in the surf with me."

Even as she sighed heavily, Duncan knew she was tempted. "What ever happened to spending the day in bed?"

"After surfing," he promised. They'd always meshed in bed. Even after that argument the night before she'd flown off to Egypt. Sometime during the night of marathon sex, Duncan had come up with a new plan to show Cass all the ways they fit perfectly together in the rest of their lives. "You'll love it."

17

CASSANDRA DID LOVE it. Loved looking at her husband in that body-hugging black wetsuit, loved the way he looked at her back, and she especially loved having his arms around her as they'd flown across the waves like Fann, a Celtic sea goddess portrayed in the Ulster Cycle, one of the great collections of ancient Irish mythology.

"That was a grand time," she said later as they warmed up back at the cottage beneath the shower. "Though I'm still not sure about the pie." He'd eaten a huge piece of berry pie topped off with a mountain of vanilla ice cream.

"You've never eaten a blueberry muffin?"

"Of course. Sedona's adding them to her menu, so I was her taste tester." They'd been delicious. And for women who weren't lucky enough to have Duncan McCaragh make love to them, probably better than a run-of-the-mill orgasm.

"Or a strawberry pancake?"

"From time to time."

"So, it could be argued, my berry pie was merely the same idea. In a different crust."

"What about the ice cream?" Cassandra knew she'd

lose ground if he brought up the equally high mountain of whipped cream topping off her pancakes.

"Dairy," he answered without missing a beat. "An important part of the food pyramid. Just like a glass of milk. Or carton of yogurt." He squeezed some body soap out of the bottle and began spreading it over her breasts. "Or that whipped cream that undoubtedly came with your strawberry pancakes."

She laughed because he had her there. And then, as his fingers slipped into her with a silky ease while the water streamed down and the room filled with fragrant steam, he had her again.

"I MAY NOT move for a week," she moaned, but in a good way, as much, much later, Duncan lay sprawled on top of her in the bed.

"That works for me." He ran his hand from her shoulders down her back over the swell of her butt. *Mine.* "There's undoubtedly someone in the village we can pay to bring us food from the pub. Or the market."

"Speaking of the village," she said, "that was really strange driving through it."

The streets, which only the day before had been filled with Lady seekers, had been nearly deserted.

"Yeah. I wonder where everyone went."

"If they'd decided to risk the curse and went to the lake, we would've seen them when we got home."

Duncan liked that she'd referred to the cottage as *home.* Liked the way her fingers were playing idly in his hair even more. The change in her from when she'd arrived at the cottage almost had him believing in all the tales of Irish magic and miracles. She'd shown up at his door looking worlds better than she had the last time he'd seen her, but along with being understandably exhausted, she'd also been tense. Edgy. And, which had given him hope, conflicted.

He'd known that if he could only buy enough time, he could rid her of that hesitance. But although he'd remained positive, he'd expected it to be a longer campaign.

He'd had another thought last night while they were at the pub. A plan that would radically change both their lives. A plan that, like her dream, actually still sounded good this morning. And even better now.

Duncan was debating whether or not to just spring it on her or let their time together wind out a bit more, when he'd have a better chance for a positive outcome, when his cell phone rang.

Having had the matter decided for him, at least for now, he reluctantly rolled off her and scooped up the phone. The number on the display was local, the last name familiar.

"Duncan McCaragh," he answered.

"Mr. McCaragh, this is Rory Joyce. I'm Michael Joyce's nephew?" In Irish fashion, his deep voice went up a little on the end of the sentence, making it sound like a question.

No wonder Joyce had been so protective of his source, Duncan thought. "It's good to hear from you. I was hoping you'd call," he said. At that, Cass sat up. From the vibes he was picking up, she'd switched from happy, sexually contented female into full reporter mode. "And the name's Duncan."

"And I'd be Rory." There was a slight pause. "Uncle Michael said you were wanting to hear about the Lady."

"I do." Duncan said carefully. "Would this be a firsthand account?"

"It would. When I was just a young lad, she was my best friend."

"And now?"

Another thoughtful pause spun out. Just when Duncan began to wonder if they'd lost the signal, Rory Joyce answered his question. "That's not a story for the phone," he said. "Would it be convenient if I visited you at the cottage?"

"Of course. I assume you know the way?"

"I do. My uncle and Bram Brennan hired me to thatch the roof last summer. I can be there in fifteen minutes, if the time suits you."

"Fifteen minutes suits me fine," Duncan agreed as Cass leaped from the bed and began scooping up scattered clothing from the floor. "I'll be looking forward to it." As his attention was momentarily distracted when she bent down to pick up her bra, he decided he could live to be a hundred and never get tired of the sight of his wife naked. "And Rory?"

"Yes, sir?"

"Thank you."

"I'll be there soon," he responded, again sounding uneasy, despite his willingness to share his story.

"You look good enough to eat," he said, rubbing his jaw as Cass shimmied beneath the bed to retrieve her underpants.

"Quit trying to seduce me and get dressed!"

"We still have time."

"He's going to smell sex on me." After she'd wiggled back out, Duncan reached down, held out a hand, and helped her back onto her feet. "You always smell great to me."

"Stop that!" She hit his chest with her palm, pushing him away. "I need a shower and you need to get dressed."

"Don't you think you're overreacting a bit?"

She was holding the clothing to her chest, unfortunately depriving him of a very fine view of her breasts. "No. I do not... Now, get dressed and go make some coffee." She dragged a hand through her tousled curls. "And of course you don't have anything decent to serve him."

"I have spaghetti and a jar of Marsala sauce."

She closed her eyes. Not in ecstasy, as she had earlier, but in obvious frustration. "Men," she huffed. "You people with penises strut around like you own the planet, but about certain things, you can be totally useless."

"That's not what you said about my penis a few minutes ago," he reminded her.

"We're wasting time." Bright spots colored her cheekbones.

"You haven't heard that old Irish saying about 'When God made time, he made plenty of it?'"

"Get dressed," she repeated, not bothering to respond to what they both knew was a rhetorical question. "Now."

She marched from the room. A moment later, he heard the water running in the shower. Which had him considering joining her.

They were down to twelve minutes. Which was doable. But since Duncan doubted that Cass was at the moment, he scooped up his jeans and T-shirt and, following in the footsteps of all the wise husbands who'd gone before him, did as his wife had instructed.

18

THERE WAS NO mistaking the family resemblance. Rory Joyce had a shock of dark hair, soulful blue-black eyes, and a scattering of freckles connecting his cheekbones over the bridge of his nose. He would, Duncan thought, look a great deal like his uncle in twenty years.

"I appreciate you taking the time to talk with me," Duncan said once introductions had been made.

"My uncle assured me that you're not one of those tabloid writers who'd be exaggerating the story and making the town, including myself, look like daft *culchie*. A country person," he defined the word before either Duncan or Cass could ask. "Usually a daft or stupid one."

"No. I wouldn't do that," Duncan assured him with a sideways glance toward Cass, who appeared unwounded by the unflattering tabloid remark. Which was easier given that her work couldn't be accused of such behavior, either.

"Would you like to sit down?" she asked, giving Duncan another of those narrowed-eyed female looks that let him know she found his social skills sorely lacking. "I'd offer you something to eat, but I'm afraid we haven't been to the market."

"No problem," Rory said. "Since I was thinking that

the story's better told at the lake."

"Which is surrounded by an impenetrable and possibly cursed briarwood hedge," Duncan pointed out.

When the young man's grin brightened those deep eyes to sapphire, the small lines that appeared at the corners of Cass's mouth suggested she was holding back a smile while thinking the same thing he was. That a young man as handsome as Rory Joyce could well be a heart-breaker.

"The lake's on my family's land," he said, seconding what Michael Joyce had mentioned last night in Brennan's. "And wouldn't we be knowing a secret passageway?"

"And you'll take us there?" Cass asked. Duncan heard the excitement in her voice.

"I will," Rory said. "If, when you write about my time with her, you don't mention the way in."

"There's no way I'd do that," Duncan assured him. While the kid seemed both smart and sane, six-year-old boys often had soaring imaginations. When he'd been in first grade, he'd stood up at the front of the room when each student introduced him or herself, and claimed he was an astronaut who'd just returned from a mission to Mars.

Maybe, he thought with wry amusement as he remembered that day, *he* was the one who should be writing for the *Worldwide Buzz*.

"I do have a question," Duncan asked.

"I'll do my best to answer it."

"What happened to the people?"

"People?" Rory's brow furrowed.

"The Lady seekers," Cass clarified.

"Ah. They went home."

"All of them? Why?"

Another furrowing of the brow. "You didn't know?"

"I guess not," Duncan said.

"She made an appearance this noon."

"You're kidding!" Cass exchanged a disbelieving look with Duncan. *While we were surfing?* it said.

"Not at all. There was quite a fuss when she suddenly rose out of the water and, although I know it's going to sound even more outlandish, appeared to be posing. She swam back and forth across the lake for about ten minutes. Then disappeared beneath the water, as she does."

"Okay." Duncan blew out a breath. "That's pretty incredible." There were also undoubtedly photographs to back the story up. Which meant that he could have some 'splaining to do to Winston Armstrong for not having taken any himself. However, if he were able to report back that he'd repaired the rift in his marriage, maybe he'd be off the hook for the lack of a firsthand Lady report.

On the other hand, there was yet another possibility he still needed to speak with Cass about. Later.

"But why would that make them leave?" Cass asked. "You'd think that even more people would be flooding to town after an actual sighting."

"There'd be no point in it," Rory said. "Given the other part of the legend."

"Which would be?" Duncan was trying not to grind his back molars to dust. Although typically he found the Irish roundabout way of speaking colorful, at the moment he wished the kid would just get to the damn point. Whatever it was.

"Once the Lady makes a public appearance, she must,

according to the myth, return to her underwater kingdom and remain there for the next three years."

"And people believe that why?"

Rory shrugged. "I'm not sure I care, since it always makes them leave."

Cassandra got it first. "It's like the hedge," she said. "Something that's been added over time to keep the village from becoming another overcrowded tourist destination."

"It could be something like that," he said with a quick grin that confirmed her accusation. Then he turned more thoughtful. "But I also suppose they believe because they want to. Myths and legends can be a powerful thing. My degree is in Irish studies, and I'll begin teaching them next fall at St. Bernadette Mary High School here in Castlelough.

"They're part of what had our society and robust education and library systems flourishing while the Europe continent became bogged down in the Dark Ages after the fall of Rome. There are some who could make a case that while the Irish perhaps didn't entirely save civilization, as some claim, we *do* possess a continual cultural and intellectual record from prehistory to current times."

"I need to talk with you," Cass said suddenly. "Not just about the Lady but about the history. I'm writing a novel, and you'd be such a wonderful source of research material."

"I'd be happy to help. And to point you to other, more august sources."

"Ah, but I *like* you," she said, making him laugh.

It did not escape Duncan's notice that Rory Joyce had proven the missing link in Cass's novel decision-making process. Just telling him about her novel had her looking like a Thoroughbred about to burst from the starting gate.

Once again he was forced to wonder at the way things kept working out even better than he could have planned.

19

THEY MADE THEIR way along the trail that Cassandra had taken earlier. Past the old cemetery and the cairn, which, hidden in the green folds of the mountain, had gone unchanged for millennia. This time, as they paused, she thought more about those early ones who'd been buried with tools, weapons, and household goods that they'd need in their next realm.

Had they found their place of resurrection? Or were their spirits still standing guard over an ancient past?

It occurred to her as they continued on that, while times might change, people didn't. Hadn't she been wandering all alone in a dark and lonely place only to have arrived here, where her once-shattered soul had found not only peace but purpose?

Her place of resurrection.

She was mulling over how to include a narrator who could meld a personal story to a legend that would then, like a continuing change, affect the lives of others who were drawn into the ever-expanding circle when they came to the towering hedge.

"It's this way," Rory Joyce said, turning to lead them through a field of blue, yellow, white, and pink flowers, many seeming to grow out of solid rock, to an opening that a person would never notice, had they not known it was there.

Rory held back a thick briarwood branch that had been concealing it with white flowers and stepped aside, allowing Cassandra, then Duncan to go before him through the fragrant passageway.

"Oh, wow." Cassandra reached for Duncan's hand as they gazed down at Lake Caislean. Surrounded by feathery-crowned reeds, the lake glistened in the sunlight like sapphire satin set on a green velvet carpet. She imagined if they'd come at night, they might have caught faeries dancing in the moonlight. "It's stunning."

"And peaceful," Duncan murmured. "A place where a person's head could slow down and catch up with his heart."

"We have a saying," Rory said, "*ciúnas gan uaigneas.* It means quietness without loneliness."

"It so fits," Cassandra said, grateful that all those Lady seekers hadn't been able to invade the sanctity of this cathedral-like place.

"Aye," Rory said. "So, before I tell you my personal connection to the Lady, I must fill you in on her backstory.

"She was once a queen whose long yellow hair flowed down her back in waves and glittered like a leprechaun's gold in the sun. She ruled over a splendid kingdom on these very shores, and because she was as benevolent as she was beautiful, the ancient gods had rewarded her people by bestowing upon them a magical gift: a sweet spring whose waters brought youth to all who drank of it."

"The Fountain of Youth," Duncan said.

"Some have made that same comparison, but we've kept the secret well as another ploy to keep us from being overrun by even more tourists.

"Not wanting the spring to flood the valley, the queen instructed that it be capped every night with a large stone. But unfortunately, a faerie who lived in the glen fell in love with the queen's handsome husband. Her sour spirit had made her as ugly as an old boar, as sharp as a brier, and as evil as the devil, which made it difficult for any man, let alone one married to such a good and lovely queen, to love her back.

"So, she turned herself into a beautiful young girl. But still the noble king remained faithful to his lady, and when he refused to return her affections, she lost her temper and cast a wicked spell on him.

"That night, during the summer solstice celebration, despite having always been a man who could hold his mead, the prince got drunk and passed out before putting the capstone on the spring."

"I can see this coming," Duncan murmured.

"Aye. It flowed and flowed, and by the time the sun rose in the morning, the entire valley, including the fairest of cities and all its people were now underwater. But, because the water was magic, no one drowned. Instead they adapted quite well to their new life below the lake. Although every so often, the queen, who sensibly replaced her fine satin gowns with waterproof emerald scales, comes to the surface to gaze upon the hills that she continues to miss after all these many years.

"And there are fishermen who swear that sometimes on a still summer evening, you can look over the edge of your boat and catch a shimmering glimpse of the turrets of the queen's castle and the townspeople busily going about their daily work."

"That's a very bittersweet story," Cassandra said.

"It is, indeed. But isn't all life comprised of both bitter and sweet? We can only hope they balance themselves out."

As he blew out a breath, Cassandra found herself holding her own. She sensed he was finally ready to tell the tale they'd come to hear. And having heard the legend, as much as her heart wanted to believe it could be true, her head, having engaged in years of fact checking, said otherwise.

"The Lady first appeared to me when I was six years old. It was a difficult time for my family. My da died in a steeplechase accident before my first birthday, leaving my mother to struggle to keep the farm going and raise both me and her younger sisters and brothers all alone.

"Although she always kept up a good front, late at night, I could hear her weeping in her room. My great-grandmother Fionna had taught us all that God always answers our prayers. But I'd been praying for what seemed like forever, and a da hadn't appeared. And my aunt Kate had given me a magical druid stone, but that hadn't helped, either."

Cass would have had to have been blind and deaf not to see the remembered sorrow in his dark eyes. To hear the helplessness of a young boy in his voice.

"Making things even worse was that we were going to have to leave Castlelough and the farm that had been in the family for centuries so my mother could take a job with a businessman in Galway."

"Moving when you're young can be difficult." And

didn't both she and Duncan know that firsthand? A lack of roots was another thing they had in common.

"I first came out here to be alone," he said. "Where I could cry without my aunt Celia catching me at it. Although she's my mother's sister, she's only a year older than me and back then liked to sport her superiority.

"One particularly bad day, I was sitting on the bank, crying my eyes out, when the Lady first appeared. At first I thought I might have dozed off in the warm sun and was dreaming. But she was as real as you or Mr. McCaragh."

"Duncan," Duncan reminded the young man quietly, as if not wanting to interrupt the narrative.

"Duncan," Rory agreed. Then sighed. "The Lady became my best friend. I'd visit every day and share anything and everything with her. Things I couldn't even share with my mother."

"Did she talk back?" Duncan, always the reporter, asked.

"Not in the beginning. But I could sense that she was listening... Which has you thinking even more that I'm either making this up or was hallucinating as a child."

"He didn't say that," Cass said.

"But he's thinking it," Rory said. "As I myself might, had I not experienced her presence. Then one day, she did speak. The words, meant to reassure me at a dark and sad time, weren't spoken out loud, but I heard them quite clearly in my head.

"Shortly after that, Quinn came to Castlelough, stayed at our house, and he and Mam fell in love. Of course, like all romances, they had their ups and downs, but they eventually got married in the circle of stones on our farm, and all our lives made a hundred-and-eighty-degree turn for the better.

"Which is when the Lady stopped appearing to me."

"Just like that?"

"Aye. I later came to the conclusion that once I no longer needed her, she either went back to staying beneath the lake or began appearing to someone else who needed an open heart who would listen to their problems.

"So. That is my tale you asked for. There are undoubtedly others in the village who've had a similar experience, though I've never had anyone tell me of it. Which makes sense because only my family knows. My grandda did claim to have seen her, but then again, he was a man fond of his drink and had also claimed to see leprechauns and faeries, so there are few who put much credence to his tales."

"Thank you," Cass said. "That was lovely, and you were very generous to share it."

"I'm glad you found it worth your time."

"Well worth it," Duncan said. "Although it's a difficult concept to wrap my mind around, you've definitely shifted my thinking."

"It's glad I am to hear that."

As he smiled, Cassandra couldn't help thinking how the teenage girls at St. Bernadette Mary High School were going to react to the newest member of the faculty. Rory Joyce, she imagined, would have more than a few personal challenges his first year of teaching. But she had no doubt that he was up to handling anything thrown his way.

20

"SO, WHAT DID you think?" Duncan asked Cass after they'd returned to the cottage and Rory had driven back to the Joyce farm. He'd told them that Quinn Gallagher had expanded the property to include guest-houses, one of which he was staying in while preparing for his new job.

"You're going to think I've been drinking the Cas-tlelough Kool-Aid, but I believe him," Cass said.

"I'm still a skeptic. But there's no way I'm going to write his story. Because while the *Castlelough Celtic* is far from a credible paper, if it picked up the story on some wire service, or worse yet, if it appeared on RTÉ, locals would be able to put two and two together and figure out who the story was about."

"Which Rory Joyce doesn't need his first year of teach-ing."

"Definitely not." So...Duncan thought about sharing his new plan with Cass. Then decided it wouldn't hurt to wait for a few hours.

They'd go to the pub. Have a pint and dinner, dance if there was music, then return home. To bed. And then, after they made love, he'd lay the idea on her.

Failure was definitely not an option. But as they drove to Brennan's, Duncan wished he'd thought to ask Rory if he still had that magical druid stone.

"I THINK YOU'VE killed me," Duncan said as he lay on his back amidst hot, tangled sheets. This time Cass was sprawled over him.

"I'm sorry." She didn't sound it. What she sounded was more than a little pleased with herself.

"That's okay. You give good sex, sweetheart. It was worth dying for." At least he'd died a happy man.

She rolled off him and lay on her back beside him. "Thank you. I think. But I don't believe dead men can talk," she said.

"Sure they can. You never saw that Willis flick?"

"Of course I did. But *The Sixth Sense* was fiction."

"Ah, but we're in Ireland. Where there's a thin line not only between realms but seemingly between fact and fiction."

"I suppose that's true enough." She turned on her side, propped herself up on an elbow, and ran a hand down his chest, to his stomach, then lower, curling her fingers around him.

"But you certainly don't feel dead."

"Don't pay any attention to that," he said as his body responded to her stroking touch. "It's stolen the blood from my brain again, and this time I'm taking back control because we need to talk."

"Oh?" She removed her hand, hitched up in bed, and

looked at him. "If it's about what I came here to discuss——
"

"No." He quickly cut her off before she could say the dreaded D word. "But it *is* about us."

Because he couldn't allow himself to be distracted, Duncan crawled out of bed, relieved to discover that his legs were still working. *Dead Man Walking.*

"I love you," he said after he'd pulled on the pair of boxer briefs he'd retrieved from where they'd landed atop the chest of drawers after Cass had ripped them off him.

"I know. I love you, too."

"But?" He didn't like the unwelcome hesitation he'd heard in her soft tone.

"I don't know. We loved each other once. And it wasn't enough."

"That was my fault."

"No." She shook her head. "It wasn't your fault. I've finally accepted it wasn't even mine. It just was what it was at the time."

"We didn't expect to be hammered like that," Duncan pointed out. "Your parents had a good marriage. From what you've told me, they were best friends who managed to be in love after all their years together."

"They were soul mates," she said. "Although having them die was the second worst time in my life, I've realized that them dying together in that earthquake was for the best. Because I'm not sure either one of them could have survived that long without the other."

"I never witnessed anything like that at home." Duncan rubbed his eyes with the heels of his hands. "I never thought it was possible to have a connection like that. Until I met you.

"Which is why I want time to show you how good we can be together, in every way, not just sex, before you pull out those papers you brought with you."

"I had a plan, too," she admitted. "To have you sign on the dotted line as soon as I got here."

"But you didn't."

"No. And not just because you asked me to wait. Because once you opened the door, I wasn't sure of anything anymore."

"Because you remembered what we'd had."

"And lost," she pointed out, making him wonder why he'd ever thought this might be easy.

"We'll make a pledge that if we start going off the rails, we'll get help," Duncan suggested. "A marriage tune-up."

Cass shook her head. "It still wouldn't work."

"Why not?"

"Because I'm no longer the woman I was. The same way I can't return to serious journalism, I can't be married to a man I only see for a few days at a time. A man who could get himself killed in some godforsaken place. It wasn't easy putting myself back together, Duncan. I'm not sure I'd have the strength to do it again if I lost you."

"You're way stronger than you think. But that's a moot point because I'm quitting."

"What?"

"I sent the e-mail to Winston this evening. Before we went to the pub, because, when I asked you to try again, I wanted you to realize that I'm willing to do whatever it takes to make things work."

"You love your work."

"I did. Now I don't. And even when I did love it, I always loved you more."

"What would you do?"

"How would you like to be married to a newspaper man?"

"Papers are closing every day. The ones that don't are going online. It's not exactly a growth industry."

"As it happens, I just happen to know a paper that's for sale. Which I could buy for a song, and with a little help from my wife, when she's not writing the great American novel, turn the thing around."

He saw the comprehension dawn in her remarkable eyes. "You're talking about the *Castlelough Celtic*."

"I am. While you were getting dressed earlier, I called the owner. It's true what Brennan said about him wanting to move to Greece. We could have it for a song."

"And live here in Castlelough?"

"And live here in Briarwood Cottage."

"Don't tell me. You also talked with Michael Joyce."

Duncan shrugged. "I'm a Marine. I plan missions. And you, Cassandra Carpenter, are the most important mission I've ever undertaken."

Her teeth were worrying her bottom lip. Something else was bothering her. Something Duncan couldn't quite get a handle on. Deciding he'd thrown enough at her for one night, he returned to the bed.

"Just think about it, okay?" He lowered his head and brushed his lips against hers. Teasing, coaxing, taking things slowly when what he wanted to do was drag her into the mists until her brain was so muddled she'd have no choice but to agree.

"I promise." She turned in his arms and framed his face between her palms. "But for the moment, I wouldn't be complaining if you were to be making love to me again," she said on a lilting brogue, sounding as if she'd grown up in this very cottage.

Unable to resist her anything, as he said good-bye to his brain yet again, Duncan willing complied.

He'd been dozing when he felt the sheets shift. Heard her pad on bare feet out of his room down the hall. Then, to his surprise, instead of her returning from the bathroom, he heard the front door open. And close with a finality that chilled Duncan's blood in the exact same way as when he'd received that call from Egypt.

21

A LTHOUGH CASSANDRA HAD retrieved the flashlight from the emergency kit that had come with her rental car, she didn't need it as a full moon lighted her way along the path past the high Celtic crosses, the mounded cairn, the wildflowers, which had closed their petals for the night, wisely sleeping as she should be doing, to the secret passageway to the lake.

When she reached it, she sat on the bank, looking out over the smooth, moonlit water, thinking of that Irish saying Rory Joyce had told them: *ciúnas gan uaigneas.* Quiet without loneliness.

Well, it was certainly quiet, without so much as a breeze sighing through the reeds. But despite Duncan sleeping only a few minutes away, she was so, so lonely.

There was a rustling sound, then the ripple of water as a magnificent creature—lough beastie, she reminded herself—rose from the glassy cobalt depths.

There's no need for you to be lonely, Cassandra Carpenter, the Lady said. As Rory had explained, she didn't say the words out loud, but Cassandra definitely heard them in her head. *You're truly and deeply loved by your man back at Briarwood Cottage.*

"I know." For some reason, Cassandra didn't feel at all foolish talking to this mythical queen who'd traded in her royal robes for scales that shone like polished emeralds in the moon dust. "But I'm afraid."

This time the Lady didn't respond. Cassandra knew that was because she was waiting for her to share the secret she'd kept hidden in her heart.

"I'd always been so brave. I felt invincible. As if I had super powers, you know?" She'd no sooner said the words than she realized who she was talking to. "Of course you do… But then I lost my baby, and everything changed. I became afraid of losing everything else in my life."

Including your husband. Duncan McCaragh.

"Yes."

Which is why you sent him away. It gave you a sense of the control you'd lost in Egypt.

Having accepted the idea of a telepathic lough beastie in the first place, Cassandra wasn't going to quibble about how the Lady might have known about that.

"Now you sound like my cousin. And Doctor Fletcher."

You've received good counsel. But the answer has always been inside your own heart, Cassandra Carpenter. Look there and you'll find your answer.

Apparently having said her piece, she gave a flick of her enormous tail and disappeared beneath the water.

"Wow." Cassandra breathed as she thought about what she'd just experienced. And knew that there was also no way she'd ever write about it.

"Wow is an understatement," a deep, wonderfully familiar voice said behind her.

She turned and watched Duncan approach.

"I'm honestly not stalking you," he said, that uncharacteristic wariness in his voice again. "I just wanted to make sure you were safe."

"I was. Am." She glanced back at the now-smooth glassy water. "I take it you saw her?"

"In all her emerald glory. Yeah. Either that or we're sharing a dream. Or a hallucination."

"Did you hear her?"

"No." He sat down beside her on the bank, bent his knees, and looped his arms over them. "I take it you did?"

"I did. And while it sounds even crazier, I think she knew that I'd be coming here tonight. And made that big showy appearance earlier to cause all those Lady seekers to leave so that she could talk to me alone."

"At this point I'm not about to call anything or anyone crazy… Are you going to share what she said?"

"Only to you… She told me that I didn't have to be lonely. That my husband, who was back at the cottage, loved me."

"A wise beastie is our Lady," Duncan said.

"She also told me that I didn't have to be afraid of losing you."

"Not going to happen," he agreed.

"And that I should look for the answer inside my heart."

"I'm not going to argue that." He lowered his legs and pulled her onto his lap. "And what is your heart telling you?"

"That I love you more than I'll ever love anyone else. That you're my other half. And that I want to spend the rest of my life with you, loving and laughing and hopefully making babies in our little thatched-roof Irish cottage."

"I'm definitely up for making babies with you." He nuzzled her neck. "Want to start now?"

She laughed. "How did I not realize I'd married a man who turns life into a series of missions?"

"I'm a Marine," Duncan told her. "It's what we do…when we're not doing this."

As they shared a slow, deep kiss, the stars spun, and the full, floating moon bathed them in silvery dust while gossamer-winged faeries danced beneath the magical light.

Meanwhile, unbeknownst to Duncan and Cass, satisfied that all was finally well, the Lady bestowed a benevolent smile on these two formerly wounded hearts before diving deeper, returning to her enchanted palace beneath the smooth, moon-spangled lake.

The End

To keep up with publication dates and other news and for a chance to win books and other cool stuff, subscribe to the JoAnn Ross newsletter. Also connect with JoAnn at her website, Facebook, Twitter, and Pinterest.

Keep reading for a sneak preview excerpt of *A Sea Change*, the next book in the Castlelough series, coming in early 2015.

A Sea Change

A Shelter Bay/Castlelough novel

JoAnn Ross

LTHOUGH THE MICROBREWERY might be a new
addition, Brennan's Microbrewery and Pub had been
serving rebels and raiders, smugglers and sailors, poets and
patriots since 1650.

And, Sedona Sullivan considered as she watched a
young couple share a kiss inside one of the two snugs by
the front door, lovers. The leaded glass window kept
people's behavior reasonably sedate while the stained glass
door allowed conversations to remain private.

Whiskey bottles gleamed like pirates' booty in the glow
of brass-hooded lamps, a turf fire burned in a large open
hearth at one end of the pub, warming against the chill of
rain pelting on the slate roof, and heavy wooden tables
were crowded onto the stone floor. Booths lined walls
covered in football flags, vintage signs, old photographs,
and in the library extension, books and magazines filled
shelves and wall racks.

The man murmured something in the woman's ear,
causing her to laugh and toss hair as bright as the peat fire.
As the woman lifted her smiling lips to his for a longer,
more drawn-out kiss, Sedona felt a stir of something that
felt uncomfortably like envy.

How long had it been since a man had made her laugh
with sexy abandon? How long since anyone had kissed her
like the man was kissing that pretty Irish redhead?

Sedona did some quick mental math. Finding the sum
impossible to believe, she recalculated. Twenty-two
months, three weeks, and eight days? Seriously?

Unfortunately, given that she was, after all, a former

CPA with excellent math skills and a near-photographic memory, Sedona knew her figures were right on the money. As where those additional sixteen hours she reluctantly tacked on to the initial subtotal.

How could that be possible?

Granted, she'd been busy. After leaving a high-powered accounting career in Portland, she'd opened a bakery in Shelter Bay, Castlelough's sister city on the Oregon coast. But still... nearly two years?

That was just too depressing.

Unlike last evening, when Brennan's had been crowded to the ancient wooden rafters with family members and close friends enjoying Mary Joyce and J.T. Douchett's rehearsal dinner, tonight the pub was nearly deserted, save for the lovers, three men watching a replay of a rugby match on the TV bolted to the stone wall, and an ancient man somewhere between eighty and a hundred years old who was nursing a foam-topped dark ale and singing sad Irish songs to himself.

And, of course, there was Patrick Brennan, owner, bartender and cook, whose smiling Irish eyes were as darkly brown as the fudge frosting she'd made for the chocolate groom's cake.

Which was what had brought Sedona to her ancestral homeland.

She'd met international movie star and award-winning screenwriter Mary Joyce when the Castlelough-born actress had visited Shelter Bay for a film festival featuring her movies. After Mary had gotten engaged to a former Marine who'd been pressed into service as a bodyguard, Mary had asked Sedona to make both the groom's cake and the all-important wedding cake.

Happy to play a part in her friend's wedding, Sedona had jumped at the chance to revisit the land of her ancestors.

A cheer went up as a player dressed in a green jersey from the Ireland Wolfhounds scored against the England Saxons. After delivering her order, Patrick paused on his way back to the bar long enough to glance up at the screen, and even the old man stopped singing long enough to raise his mug before switching to a ballad celebrating a victory in some ancient, but never to be forgotten war.

Sedona was thinking that watching a game when you already knew the final score must be a male thing, when the heavy oak door opened, bringing with it a wet, brisk wind that sent her paper napkin sailing off her lap and onto the floor.

Before she could reach down and pick it up, her attention was captured by the arrival of a man she had already determined to be trouble on a hot, sexy stick.

His wind-mussed hair, which gave him the look of having just gotten out of bed, fell to a few inches above his broad shoulders and was as black as the sea on a moonless night. As he took off his black leather jacket—revealing a lean hard, well-muscled body—testosterone radiated off him in bone-weakening waves that had her glad she was sitting down.

"Well, would you look at what the night gale blew in," Patrick greeted him from behind the bar. "I thought you were leaving town."

"I was. Am," Conn Brennan clarified in the roughened, gravelly rocker's voice recognizable the world over. "I'm flying out of Shannon to catch up with the lads in Frankfurt. But I had a sudden craving for fish and chips and sure, everyone knows there's no finer food than the pub grub served up by my big brother at Brennan's."

Patrick laughed at that. "Sure, with talk like that, some would think you'd be from Blarney," he shot back on an exaggerated brogue. "So how did the party go? I assume the bride and groom enjoyed themselves?"

"The party was grand, in large part due to the music," Conn Brennan said. The infamous bad boy rocker known by the single name *Conn* to his legion of fans around the world had been dubbed "Conn of the Hundred Battles" by tabloids for his habit for getting into fights with the paparazzi.

"As for the happy bride and groom, I image they're shagging their brains out about now. The way they couldn't keep their hands off each other had the local band lads making bets on whether they'd make it to bed before consummating the nuptials."

The heels of his metal-buckled black boots rang out on the stone floor as he headed toward the bar, pausing when he almost stepped on Sedona's dropped napkin. He bent to pick it up, then, when he straightened, his startlingly neon blue eyes clashed with hers.

And held for a long, humming moment.

"Well, fancy seeing you here. I would have guessed, after the busy day you've had, that you'd be all tucked away in your comfy bed at the inn, dreaming of wedding cakes, sugar plums, and all things sweet."

He placed the napkin on the table with a dangerously sexy smile he'd directed her way more than once as he'd rocked the reception from the bandstand. When an image of a bare-chested Conn, sprawled on her four-poster bed at the inn flashed wickedly through Sedona's mind, something quivered deep in her stomach.

It was only hunger, she assured herself. Between putting the last touches on the towering wedding cake and working with the serving staff during the reception, she hadn't taken time for a proper meal all day.

"I was in the mood for a glass of wine and a late bite." Her tone, cool as wintry mist over the Burren, was in direct contrast to the heat flooding her body.

He lifted an ebony brow. "Why would you be wanting to go out in this rain? The Cooper Beech Inn has excellent room service, and surely your suite came with a mini-bar well stocked with adult beverages."

"You're correct on both counts," she acknowledged as the old man segued into "The Rare Auld Mountain Dew."

She took a sip of wine, hoping it would cool the heat rising inside her.

It didn't.

"But I chose to spend my last night in Ireland here at Brennan's instead of an impersonal hotel room. Besides, you're right about your brother's food. It's excellent."

While the pub grub menu might be more casual than her chef friend Maddy Douchett's gourmet dining, Patrick Brennan had proven to be as skilled in the kitchen as he was pulling pints. "There's also the fact that the mini bar is ridiculously expensive."

"Ah." He nodded his satisfaction. "Your parents didn't merely pass down an Irish surname, Sedona Sullivan. It appears you've inherited our Irish frugality."

"And here I thought that was the Scots."

"It's true that they've been more than happy to advertise that reputation, despite having stolen the concept from us. Same as they did the pipes, which, if truth be told, were originally intended as an Irish joke on the Scots, who, being dour people without any sense of humor, failed to get it."

"And didn't I recognize your famed Irish frugality the moment you roared into town in that fire-engine red Ferrari?"

He threw back his head and laughed, a rich, deep, sound that flowed over her and reminded her yet again exactly how much time had passed since she'd been with a man.

Your choice.

"And wouldn't you be a prime example of appearances being deceiving, Sedona Sullivan?" he countered.

"Don't be disturbing my guests, Conn," Patrick called out.

"We're just having a friendly conversation." Conn's eyes hadn't left Sedona's since he'd stopped at the table. "Am I disturbing you, *a stór?*"

Yes.

"Not at all," she lied.

The truth was that she'd been feeling wired and edgy from the moment he strode into the hall for a sound check before the reception.

"Though you do force me to point out that I'm no one's *darling,*" she tacked on. He'd undoubtedly used the generic endearment the way American men used "babe" or "sweetheart."

Even without having read about all the rich and fa-mous women the rocker was reported to have been involved with, any sensible woman would keep her distance from Conn Brennan. Despite having grown up in a commune of former hippies and flower children, Sedona had always considered herself unwaveringly sensible.

Her knowledge of the endearment failed to put a dent in his oversized male ego. Instead, amusement danced in his electric blue eyes.

"Would you have learned that bit of Irish from some local lad attracted by your charms?" he asked as he rubbed a jaw darkened with a day-old stubble that added machismo to his beautiful face. "Which, may I say, despite your short time in our fair village, would not surprise me in the least."

"My parents believe everyone should speak at least two languages," she responded mildly. "I'm fluent in Spanish, know enough just French to order a baguette and wine in Paris, and thanks to a year studying abroad at Trinity College Dublin, along with the past few days having an opportunity to practice, I can carry on a bit of a conversation in Irish."

Raindrops glistened in his black hair as he tilted his head. "Mary wasn't exaggerating when she was going on about your charms," he said finally. "And aren't brains and beauty an enticing combination? As for you not being my *darling*, Sedona Sullivan, the night's still young."

"Perhaps not for those in Dublin or Cork," she said, struggling against the seductive pull of that smile. The rugby game ended with a score by the redshirted Saxons. The men who'd been watching the TV shuffled out, muttering curses about allegedly blind referees. "But if you don't leave soon, you won't be able to drive your fancy 'frugal' import to the airport because Castlelough's cobblestone streets will have been rolled up."

He gave her a longer, considering look, his intense blue eyes narrowing as he scrutinized her in silence for what seemed like forever, even as some part of her brain still managing to function told her must have only been a few seconds.

"You're order's up," he said, without having even glanced toward the bar. "Since Patrick's occupied with my fish and chips, I'll bring your late bite back with my ale."

He smelled so amazing, like night rain darkened with the scent of leather and the tang of sweat from having played as hard for a small-town home crowd of a hundred wedding guests as he had to his recent sell-out crowd of ninety thousand in London's Wembley Stadium.

Tamping down a reckless urge to lick his dark neck, Sedona forced a slight smile.

"Thank you. We certainly wouldn't want your fish to burn while your brother's distracted delivering my meal."

Assuring herself that there wasn't a woman on the planet who'd be capable of not checking out the very fine butt in those dark jeans, she watched his long, lose-hipped outlaw's stride to the bar.

Not wanting to be caught staring as she he returned with his dark ale and her plate, she turned her gaze back to the couple in the snug. The woman was now sitting on the man's lap as they tangled tonsils.

Why didn't they just get a damn room?

"Now there's a pair who know how to make the most of a rainy night," Conn said as he sat down across from her.

There was no way she was going to respond to that.

Instead, she turned her attention to the small white plate of deep-fried cheese served on a bed of salad greens with a side of dark port and berry sauce. The triangular piece of cheese that had been fried in a light-as-a-feather beer batter nearly made her swoon.

As she'd discovered when making her cakes, Irish dairy farmers seemed to possess a magic that churned milk into pure gold. "This is amazingly delicious."

"The French claim they make the best cream and butter, but I'd put ours against theirs any day. That St. Brigid's cheese you're eating is a local Camembert from Michael Joyce's farm."

Michael was Mary Joyce's older brother. Sedona had met the former war correspondent turned farmer and his American wife at a dinner at the Joyce family home her first night in Castlelough.

"And speaking of delicious, I'm remiss in not telling you that your cake had me tempted to lick my plate."

"Thank you." When his words brought back her earlier fantasy of licking his neck, she felt color rising in her cheeks.

"Of course, I wouldn't have," he continued, thankfully seemingly unaware of her wicked, too tempting thoughts. "Because I promised Mary."

"You promised Mary you wouldn't lick your dessert plate?"

"No. Despite being an international movie star, Mary can be a bit of a stickler for propriety. So I promised to behave myself."

He waited a beat, just long enough to let her know something else was coming. "Which was the only reason I didn't leave a set to the lads and dance with you at the reception."

"Well, no one can fault you for your confidence."

"Would you be saying you wouldn't have given me a dance? If I hadn't been performing and had asked?"

Dance with this man? From the way he'd watched her from the bandstand, his eyes like blue flames, Sedona had a feeling that dancing wasn't precisely what he'd had in mind.

"I came here to work," she said. "Not dance." Nor hook up with a hot Irish musician.

"It was a grand cake," he said. "Even better than the one I was served at the White House." Where he'd received a presidential medal for his social activism, Sedona remembered. "And one of the few that tasted as good as it looked. Most cakes these days seem to have Spackle spread over them."

She laughed at the too true description. "That's fondant, which creates a smoother surface to decorate."

"It's shite is what it is. When I was growing up, my mam's carrot cake always won first prize at the count fair. With six children in the family, we'd all have to wait our turn to lick the bowl or she'd never have ended up with enough frosting to cover it, but I always believed that the cream cheese frosting was the best part."

Sedona was relieved when Patrick arrived at the table with his brother's fish and chips, interrupting a conversation that had returned to licking.

"Something we can agree on," she said, dipping the cheese into a sauce brightened with flavors of ginger, orange, and lemons. "Which is why I used buttercream on the cakes for the wedding."

He bit into the battered cod. Heaven help her, somehow the man managed to make chewing sexy. "So," he said, after taking a drink of the dark Brian Boru Black Ale microbrew. "Mary tells me you make cupcakes back in America."

"My bakery, *Take the Cake*, specializes in cupcakes, but I've also added pies."

"Good business move," he said with a nod. "Who wouldn't be liking a nice warm piece of pie? Cakes are well enough, but pies are sexy."

Said the man who obviously had sex on the mind. Unfortunately, he wasn't alone. As she watched him bite into a chip, she found herself wondering how that black face scruff would feel on her breasts. Her stomach. And lower still.

"Well, they're proven popular," she said as her pulse kicked up. "Which was rewarding, given that it proved the validity of months of research."

He cocked his head. "You researched whether or not people liked pie?"

"Well, of course I already knew they liked pie. I merely did a survey and cost analysis to calculate the cost and profit margins."

"Which told you lots of people like pie."

He was laughing at her. She could see it in his eyes. "Yes. Do you realize how many businesses fail on any given year? Especially these days?" They were finally in a conversational territory she knew well.

"Probably about as many people who don't succeed in the music business," he guessed. "Though I've never done a study before writing a song."

"That's different."

"Is it, now?"

"What if you wrote a song that didn't connect with your fans?"

He shrugged and took another bite of battered cod. "I'd write it off as a mistake and move on. No risk, no reward. I tend to go with my gut, then don't look back."

"My father's the same way," she murmured, more to herself than to him.

He leaned back in the wooden chair and eyed her over the rim of his glass. "And how has that worked out for him?"

"Very well, actually."

He lifted the glass. "Point made."

"Different strokes," she argued.

"You know what they say about opposites." His gaze moved slowly over her face, his eyes darkening to a stormy, deep sea blue as they settled on her lips, which had parts of her tingling that Sedona had forgotten could tingle.

"I have a spreadsheet," she said.

"I suspect you have quite a few." When he flashed her a slow, badass grin she suspected had panties dropping across several continent, Sedona sternly reminded herself that she'd never—ever—been attracted to bad boys.

So why had she forgotten how to breathe?

As that fantasy of him sprawled in her bed next door in the Copper Beach Inn came crashing to the forefront of her mind, Sedona thought of those twenty-two months, three weeks, eight days and sixteen, no almost seventeen hours.

Even if she hadn't been coming off a very long dry spell, every instinct she possessed told her that not only was Conn Brennan trouble, he was way out of her league.

"They're not all business related. I also have one for men."

Putting his ale down, he leaned across the small round table and tucked a strand of blonde hair, which had fallen from the tidy French twist she'd created for the reception, behind her ear. The brush of his fingertips, roughened from guitar strings, caused heat to rise beneath the erotic touch.

"You put us men in boxes." His eyes somehow managed to look both hot and amused at the same time.

It was not a question. But Sedona answered it anyway. "Not men. Attributes," she corrected. "What I'd require, and expect, in a mate."

Oh, God. Why did she have to use that word? While technically accurate, it had taken on an entirely different, impossibly sexy meaning. Desperately wanting to bury her flaming face in her palms, she remained frozen in place as his treacherous finger traced a trail of sparks around her lips, which, despite Ireland's damp weather, had gone desert dry.

"And where do I fit in your tidy little boxes, Sedona Sullivan?"

Although she was vaguely aware of the couple leaving the snug, and the pub, his steady male gaze was holding her hostage. She could not look away.

"You don't."

"I'm glad to hear that," he said on that deep, gravelly voice that set off vibrations like a tuning fork inside her.

Conn ran his hand down her throat, his thumb skimming over her pulse, which leaped beneath his touch, before cupping her jaw. "Because I've never been comfortable fenced into boundaries."

And growing up in a world of near-absolute freedom, Sedona had never been comfortable without them. "There's something you need to know."

"And that would be?"

"I'm not into casual sex."

"And isn't that good to hear." He lowered his mouth to within a whisper of hers. "Since there'd be nothing casual about how you affect me."

She drew in a sharp breath, feeling as if she were standing on the edge of the towering cliff where J.T. and Mary's wedding had taken place in a circle of ancient stones.

"I'm taking you back to your room."

Somehow, her hand had lifted to his face. "Your flight…"

He parted her lips with the pad of his thumb. "It's my plane. It takes off when I'm ready." His other hand was on her leg, his fingers stroking the inside of her thigh through the denim of the jeans she'd put on after returning to her room after the reception. "I'll ring up the pilot and tell him I'll be leaving in the morning."

Then his mouth came down on hers and Conn was kissing her, hard and deep, setting off a blind-blinding supernova inside her.

They left the pub, running through the soft Irish rain into the inn next door. As the old fashioned gilt cage elevator cranked its way up to her floor, he continued to kiss her breathless, making Sedona forgot that she'd never, *ever*, been attracted to bad boys.

Other books in the Castlelough series:

A Woman's Heart

Fair Haven

Legends Lake

The Shelter Bay (Castlelough's sister city) series:

The Homecoming

One Summer

On Lavender Lane

Moonshell Beach

Sea Glass Winter

Castaway Cove

Christmas in Shelter Bay (Cole and Kelli's pre-novella in A Christmas on Main Street)

You Again, coming November 11, 2014

The Shelter Bay spin-off Murphy Brothers Trilogy:

River's Bend

About The Author

When *New York Times* bestselling contemporary romance author JoAnn Ross was seven years old, she had no doubt whatsoever that she'd grow up to play center field for the New York Yankees. Writing would be her backup occupation, something she planned to do after retiring from baseball. Those were, in her mind, her only options. While waiting for the Yankees management to call, she wrote her first novella—a tragic romance about two star-crossed Mallard ducks—for a second grade writing assignment.

The paper earned a gold star. And JoAnn kept writing.

She's now written around one hundred novels (she quit keeping track long ago) and has been published in twenty-six countries. Two of her titles have been excerpted in *Cosmopolitan* magazine and her books have also been published by the *Doubleday, Rhapsody, Literary Guild*, and *Mystery Guild* book clubs. A member of the Romance Writers of America's Honor Roll of best-selling authors, she's won several awards.

Although the Yankees have yet to call her to New York to platoon center field, JoAnn figures making one out of two life goals isn't bad.

Currently writing her Shelter Bay and River's Bend series set in Oregon, where she and her husband grew up, and her Castlelough Irish series—from where her grandparents emigrated and one of her favorite places to visit—JoAnn lives with her husband and two rescued dogs (who pretty much rule the house) in the Pacific North-west.

Sign up to receive the latest news from JoAnn
http://joannross.com/newsletter

Visit JoAnn's Website
http://www.joannross.com/

Like JoAnn on Facebook
https://www.facebook.com/JoAnnRossbooks

Follow JoAnn on Twitter
https://twitter.com/JoAnnRoss

Follow JoAnn on Goodreads
www.goodreads.com/author/show/31311.JoAnn_Ross

Follow JoAnn on Pinterest
http://pinterest.com/JoAnnRossBooks

CPSIA information can be obtained at www.ICGtesting.com
Printed in the USA
LVOW11s1023161215

466838LV00002B/83/P